Seeing God in Your Story

*A journey of imagination
with sixteen women of the Bible*

Nico Richie

K. Lynn Lewis, *Managing Editor*

NEHEMIAH
PRESS

EQUIP PEOPLE FOR HIS GOOD WORKS

Katy, Texas

Print ISBN-13: 978-1-967465-02-6
Digital ISBN: 978-1-967465-03-3
Library of Congress Control Number: 2025937551

Cover design, interior design, and layout by K. Lynn Lewis. Cover photo credit TaraFlannery.com. Chapter header images used via Pro License through Vecteezy, unless otherwise credited.

Published by Nehemiah Press
NehemiahPress.com
Katy, Texas

Dedication

To the honor and glory of God,
and all my sisters who desire an
authentic relationship with God.

Contents

Acknowledgements

I am grateful and indebted to my mother who knew and loved me as only a mother can.

I am thankful for my three children, whom I love and bless. You continue to teach me more that I could ever teach you.

To my brother, my life would not be the same without you. I'm glad you are my brother.

Thank you to my three Writing Group partners who challenge me to grow spiritually as we write together.

Thank you, Dr. K. Lynn Lewis and Nehemiah Press, for believing in me and supporting my vision to bring the women of the Bible to life.

Thank you to my extended family, friends, and truly everyone I meet along life's journey. You enrich my understanding of God and show me how loving, kind, and ever-present God is in my life and in yours. We journey together!

Introduction

We met at a theatre in London. Each embracing a free afternoon, we both bought tickets to a matinee and discovered ourselves sitting next to each other watching *The Importance of Being Earnest* (2002).[1] Though strangers, we enjoyed an instant connection and, with more time, would have spent the rest of the day together as new friends, drawn from different worlds into a brief communal experience.

Sharing our stories is illuminating. We exchange parts of our life, get to know one another, discover common ground, and better understand ourselves. These fractions of our life, drawn together, reveal inherent beauty and messiness. We see where we came from and how that matters to where we are going—our looking back helps us look forward.

Seeing God in Your Story offers a shared journey of sanctified imagining with sixteen women of the Bible. Written from fictional first-person perspectives with biblical and historical insights, I pray that God will guide you as you

---

[1] A 2018 stage production at Vaudeville Theatre on The Strand in London, England and based on the 1895 play by Oscar Wilde, "The Importance of Being Earnest," billed as a trivial comedy for serious people.

1

immerse yourself in their stories—real women from real places in time and history. May they become real to you through these sketches in blank spaces embellished with colorful details. May you see God through their eyes and may He open your heart and mind to see Him and His love in your own life.

Through these sweet sixteen narratives, perhaps you will discover a person you never knew or take a refreshing look at a familiar tale. Let these women speak to you. Who knows? Though seemingly random strangers meeting in the theater of life, you may find that you have something meaningful in common.

Each chapter dives into the life of a woman in the Bible, followed by an opportunity to:

- **Explore** relevant Bible verses.
- **Reflect** through open-ended questions.
- **Imagine** through guided prayer.

Notes at the end of the book offer links for deeper study into more about the women and their circumstances.

My prayer is that as you see yourself in God's story, you will see God in your own story and see His glory in your story!

Nico Richie
March 2025

Let the redeemed of the Lord tell their story.

Psalm 107:2a (NIV)

Chapter 1
A Promise Kept

Sarah's Journey

When my spirit felt weak within me, you knew my path.
Psalm 142:3a (NASB)

A comfortable life? An easy path that avoided slippery slopes and common pitfalls? I suspect my surroundings do exude a peaceful appearance that suggests a carefree existence, and that my luxurious possessions create an illusion of wealth obtained through little effort of my own. Exotic jewelry adorns my neck, gemstone rings embellish my fingers, and soft woolen carpets decorate my home. My appearance does tell a tale, but like my aging figure, my story has wrinkles. Beyond what you see, hear my words. Over a lifespan in numerous places, I spent much of my time chasing a promise.

I grew up in the bustling and vibrant city of Ur, a thousand miles from where I am now—my probable final resting place, Kiriath Arba, also known as Hebron. In Ur, our family enjoyed both the rich blessings of an extensive, prosperous family and the modern conveniences of city life. We belonged to a sizeable clan of merchants engaged in buying, selling, and trading valuable goods with other merchants passing through our famous city. As the steady and never-ending flow of caravans passed from east to west and back again, our clan acquired wealth and status over many generations. I truly enjoyed the most splendid comforts of prosperity.

The nearby Euphrates River provided an abundance of life-giving water for everything we needed and desired. Desperate travelers who survived the trek across the parched countryside hurried to our city to find refreshment on the banks of the river and in our thriving city. Water in the desert is wealth, and we had water and wealth in abundance!

Yet long before traders and nomads reached the river's edge, they marveled at our advanced architecture. The massive Ziggurat of Ur loomed large against the desert sky. Rising effortlessly from the surrounding barren landscape, the tower served as a tall landmark in a flat terrain beckoning people to Ur—the oasis we called home. Rising atop a large terrace, the temple attracted superstitious worshippers who, at times, swelled the population of our city to capacity. They exported legendary stories of Ur, and we delighted in our reputation as one of the world's greatest cities. At the time, we also worshiped the gods of Ur, and were equally impressed by our city, our gods, and ourselves.

Although we had no children, my husband Abram and I enjoyed a good life together in the famous city where everyone wanted to go! But after his brother, Haran, died, Abram's father Terah told Abram, his brother Nahor, and Haran's son Lot to gather their people and pack their things.

"We are leaving Ur and moving to Canaan," Terah announced.

That was the worst day of my life, up to that point. Why leave Ur? Abandoning a modern, thriving city to go someplace only God knows where more than a thousand miles away? It didn't make sense to me. Plus, I still hoped to enjoy adding to my clan in Ur. Although we were not yet parents, Abram and I desperately wanted children. I longed for motherhood—a shared experience within marriage and an entire clan. What hope would we have to deliver a healthy child in a distant wilderness? I didn't know Canaan. As far as I knew, nobody in Canaan knew me, my husband, or anybody else in our family. How could I raise a child without the support of my home community?

My cauldron of emotions boiled over. I confronted Abram, attacked him with questions and accusations, and told him he didn't care about my feelings or what I wanted. He just listened. When I finally exhausted all my arguments, he simply stated, "We are leaving with Father Terah. Let's pack up our people and precious possessions and move on together." I was not particularly comforted.

We soon left our home and vibrant life behind, traveling the main road in the direction of the setting sun. Abram's compass says we traveled northwest, but I felt lost. After about 600 miles, we stopped in the trading city of Harran. Terah liked it, Nahor and his family seemed to really like it, so we ended up settling there for a while.

Though smaller than Ur, Harran was better than living in a wilderness—a lot better. We went right into the family business, lived comfortably, but Abram and I remained childless. I comforted myself in knowing that when we did have a child, at least we had family in Harran.

However, just as the loss of Abram's brother in Ur, his father's passing in Harran at the age of 205 reminded us that death is a natural part of life. I thought we might return to Ur, but Abram informed me that he received a message from the Lord, the one true God. I didn't expect that, nor did I understand. Honestly, his announcement stunned me, and I listened as he explained that we were supposed to leave our country and people, go to a land somewhere that this Lord would show us, that Abram would become a great nation, and we would bless and be blessed. He insisted that we continue our original intention to journey on to Canaan.

Land? Great nation? He seemed obsessed and determined. I tried to sort his words out in my mind.

But what good is land? And what nation? We didn't have any children, not even one. What good is land without a family to share it? Shouldn't we have children first, raise them around family and friends, and then go seek a land inheritance if we must?

It all seemed backwards. Even so, Lot accepted Abram's vision, and we packed up, left Nahor and his wife Milkah behind, and headed "south" as Abram described it.

Believe me, I know exactly what people mean when they say that something went from bad to worse! Abram tried to comfort me, reiterating that the Lord promised us land and that we would become a great nation, a blessed name, bless others, and even bless everybody in the whole world, he said. While Abram delighted in his faith, I—ashamedly in retrospect—wallowed in childless misery. And what hope did I have? When we left Harran, Abram was 75 years old; I was 65. By anyone's standards, my womb was as good as dead. What naivete, it seemed, that we could be parents of even one child, much less the matriarch and patriarch of a family. And great nation? Ha! Ha, ha, ha! Not even funny!

But we chased the promises. At times, I felt comfort amidst our little tribe, while other times I felt weighed down by the animals, people, and carts brimming with accumulated possessions. After we crossed the Euphrates River on the main road toward Egypt, we finally arrived in Canaan. We pitched our tents in a broad valley surrounded by steep hills near the city of Shechem, about 400 miles from Harran.

Life was hard, we were strangers in a strange land and we once again fell short of the promise. Our hopes for a thriving new life were crushed when a severe famine hit the area and drove us much further south where we sought refuge and survival in the prosperous nation of Egypt. We were alive but imperiled in an unfamiliar land surrounded by more unfamiliar people and customs. At that point, our hope in the promises of the Lord seemed so distant.

I must pause and confess that many have considered me beautiful. Such a gift, but also, at times, bordering on a curse. Abram thinking I was beautiful at my advanced age was wonderful. But he also thought Pharaoh—the king of Egypt—might snatch me away and take me as one of his wives! For protection, Abram convinced me to go along with the ruse that I was Abram's sister, not his wife.

"Pharaoh will kill me to get to you," he warned. He reasoned that we had to protect our hope and promises. Otherwise, if Pharaoh eliminated Abram, we could never become the great nation the Lord God promised. I agreed and hoped for some positive resolution.

As anticipated, Pharaoh brought me into his palace to prepare for marriage. Meanwhile, not only did Pharaoh spare

Abram, but he also bestowed abundant gifts on his expected new brother-in-law. Abram's wealth increased—sheep, cattle, servants, silver, gold, and precious gems—at my expense.

Unfortunately, things did not go well for Pharoah. Though innocently unaware of my marital status, the Lord inflicted diseases on Pharoah's household as punishment for his intentions. Fear reigned in the palace and he soon found out the truth about our deceit. Furious, he sent us away, along with all the riches he had given Abram, to hopefully cleanse his household from all their afflictions.

"Take your wife and go!" he shouted as he directed his men to help us pack and make sure we left Egypt.

So, once again we set out for Canaan, but this time with an even smaller flicker of hope in the promise of our own land and a national legacy. We returned with even more treasures and servants than when we first left Ur. Yet, the treasure brought little comfort. I felt emptier than ever—my womb was still barren and I could barely imagine a stable home and children of our own.

We meandered to different places, including back to Bethel, but then finally settled by the great trees of Mamre near Hebron. After leaving Harran, going to Canaan, Egypt, and then back to Canaan, we were trying to start all over again, again!

During those ten or so years, I gradually resigned myself to the grim reality that I—me personally, my body—would never bear the child that the Lord promised to Abram. I was in my seventies by then and had clearly passed well beyond the age of bearing a child.

When the Lord spoke to my husband again in a vision and repeated the same promises, Abram suggested to the Lord that a servant in our household could become his heir since we had no children of our own.

But the Lord reiterated that "a son who is your own flesh and blood will be your heir" and took Abram outside and said, "Look up at the sky and count the stars—if indeed you can count them. So shall your offspring be."

Abram believed the Lord, as well as the promise, again, of this land. It didn't make sense to me, but the more I thought about it, an idea began to form. My failure to produce an heir weighed extremely heavily on me. I was obsessed with my own dreams and Abram's visions and I kept trying to figure out how to solve my pain and fulfill the Lord's promise myself.

What about Hagar, my Egyptian servant? If she had a child, that child could be considered my child. So, if I couldn't have a child, then she could have a child for me, for Abram, for us, and thus fulfill the Lord's promise!

So, I offered Abram my servant Hagar in my stead, and he took her as his second wife. She quickly got pregnant, making it crystal clear that I was the problem, not Abram, and not the Lord. Along with her pregnancy came disdain, contempt for me and for the barrenness of my womb. I responded by complaining to my husband and mistreating her. Things got so bad she ran away, but after the angel of the Lord appeared to her in the wilderness, she returned to us and resumed her place as my servant—my now pregnant servant.

Shortly after we celebrated Abram's 86th birthday, Hagar gave birth to Ishmael. The boy delighted us, especially his father, but shadows continued to flicker across my weary soul. I failed Abram, failed the Lord, failed myself. I tried to adjust to the consequences of my choice. I tried to cope with the reality of living in tents surrounded by an open landscape, a wealth of livestock and treasure, and a growing child in my household who was not my own. My reality seemed so distant from the dreams of a younger me back in Ur, even in Harran.

After Abram turned 99 years old, the Lord appeared to him again and reiterated his promises with even more details. He changed Abram's name to Abraham, which means "father of many nations," and told Abraham to call me "Sarah," which means "mother of many nations" even though I was nearly 90 years old at the time. My husband thought it was a bit ludicrous, and laughed to himself, but the Lord insisted he was serious.

"Your wife Sarah will bear you a son, and you will call him Isaac," the Lord said. He promised it would happen by the same time next year.

This was all too impossible for me to believe, and not funny, if you want to know the truth. *Father and mother of many nations?*

We loved the reaffirmation of incredible promises, but we also felt perplexed. Both of us had a lot to learn about what it meant when God made a promise. We realized later that a promise from the Lord without a timetable did NOT require us to create one or strategize on how to fulfill a promise by ourselves. But we didn't understand those things at the time.

Not long afterwards, three men showed up midday outside our tent. We served them a meal and offered the same generous hospitality that we would offer our closest and dearest family. While they were eating I was listening from inside the tent behind them.

They asked about me and then one of them said that he would return next year and I would have a son. Next year I would be 90 and Abraham 100 years old! Such an outrageous claim struck me as funny and I laughed quietly to myself. Yet, remarkably, that was the same message Abraham said the Lord reaffirmed to him earlier. At our ages, could we as a couple even imagine that pleasure! It just didn't make sense. But again, we had a lot to learn about God's promises.

When asked why I laughed, I lied and insisted that I didn't laugh. But somehow, the Lord knew and told me so. I know he knew because it was true, and that unnerved me. Even more scary, the cities down in the Arabah where Lot and his family were living were dramatically destroyed the next day and our tribe ended up moving to Gerar for a while.

Again, history repeated itself when we were faced with a serious threat, this time from the king of Gerar, Abimelech. Just like in Egypt, worried that my beauty would catch the eye of a ruler who would snatch me away and harm us, we resorted to the ruse that I was Abraham's sister.

In truth, Terah was our father, but we had different mothers. We married within our clan according to our customs to protect ourselves from outside threats. Yes, I was Abraham's sister, but more accurately his half-sister. When we first embarked on our travels long ago, Abraham told me the way I could show my love for him was to tell everyone wherever we went that he was my brother. My heart and mind naturally objected to this half-truth; I was Abraham's wife and to say I was just his sister was a lie. I felt sad and angry at the same time! I wished Abraham would stand up for me, defend me, and defend our marriage, but he was afraid.

Also, we didn't pray about it and ask the Lord to show us a better way, which I now regret. Looking back, I can see how often my plans ended up with unwanted and unintended consequences that harmed us and other people. But, at the time, Abraham reminded me of God's promises and that the plan worked, at least for us, in Egypt.

As anticipated, King Abimelech sent for me and took me into his household. And, as in Egypt, God miraculously intervened. Although he had not yet come near me, Abimelech suffered a terrifying nightmare in which God revealed to him that I was married, Abraham was a prophet, and that Abimelech and everyone who belonged to him would die if he did not return me to Abraham and rectify the injustice. Every woman in his household was already experiencing infertility as punishment, and his dream indicated it was clearly about to get way worse. Furious with us and afraid of God, Abimelech immediately returned me to Abraham, asked Abraham to pray for him and his family, and heaped sheep, cattle, slaves, and 1000 shekels of silver upon us to cover the unintended offense.

However, unlike in Egypt where we were sent out of the country, Abimelech offered us the option to live in his land anywhere we wanted. This was an unexpected turn of events. Was God working through this person to grant us promised land? It sure seemed that way.

After this harsh and traumatic life lesson, we felt regret, and confusion about the truth and lies that haunted us as we tried to fulfill God's promises ourselves. We struggled to make sense of how our fears and doubts kept resolving themselves to our benefit. We now had a son, Ishmael, and we had land. But what of the nearly 25-year-old promise—recently reaffirmed on at least two occasions—that we ourselves would become the father and the mother of a great nation? Was it still true that Abram and Sarai would truly become Abraham and Sarah and have a son named Isaac?

Miraculously, I soon found myself pregnant and gave birth to a son. Our son. And we indeed named him "Isaac," which means "he laughs," which was appropriate since my husband and I had both laughed at such an incredulous idea. I could hardly believe it myself, not just that the impossible could happen, but that it could happen to me!

At the ripe old ages of 100 and 90, God did for us what we could have never done for ourselves. We finally began to understand that when God made promises, HE would keep HIS promises in HIS way in HIS time. We only had to believe, and trust, and wait.

Yes, wait, which was probably the hardest part. Twenty-five years is a long time to wait on any promise, much less multiple promises. Maybe we gave up too easily, and we certainly gave in to fear too often. We lied, we conspired, and we tried to do things in our own feeble power to face threats of famine and foreign rulers to protect our precious dreams and promises. In hindsight, maybe our own behavior extended the timeline; perhaps God would have fulfilled His promises earlier without our illicit interference. How childish of us. Yet, in HIS mercy, the Lord kept HIS promises despite OUR doubts and wayward behaviors.

Through our journey, we learned that God is faithful even when we are not. His faithfulness is eternal and derives from Him, not us. Despite our clever and misaligned plans, God kept an eye on us and protected us and others from our wayward actions. He kept His promises, not because of who we were or are, but because of who He is and always will be.

As Isaac—our miraculous son of promise—grew, we determined to teach him the ways of faithfulness to the Lord Almighty. We confessed our doubts and failings, and professed God's blessings and faithfulness. We boasted of God's truth and trustworthiness, and warned of temptations toward misdirected, misguided, and self-centered actions.

At this point, Isaac has rich examples of how to trust in God and His promises. We pray that he will follow our good examples and not the bad ones all his days and always trust God to keep His promises knowing that He who promises is faithful!

Explore

- *Joshua 24:2* | Abram's family does not know the God of the Bible while living in Ur.

- *Genesis 11:27–12:9* | Sarai and Abram leave home pursuing the promise of God.

- *Genesis 12:10–13:1* | Fleeing to Egypt, Abram hatches a lie, and they survive Pharaoh.

- *Genesis 16:1–4* | Sarai gives up on having her own child.

- *Genesis 17:1–8, 15–22* | God promises Abraham a child with Sarah. Abraham laughs.

- *Genesis 18:10–15* | God promises Sarah a child within the year. Sarah laughs.

- *Genesis 20* | Returning to Canaan Abraham revisits the lie; they survive King Abimelech.

- *Genesis 20:12* | SPOILER ALERT: Abraham and Sarah are half-brother and sister.

- *Genesis 21:1–6* | At the appointed time, Sarah gives birth to their son.

- *Hebrews 10:23* | God is faithful to keep His promise.

Reflect

- How much do the promises of God depend on us?

- When it comes to how we live our lives, what is our part and what is God's part?

- Did Isaac obey his parents' teaching? Did he follow their example? See Genesis 26: 1–11.

Imagine

Abram had an ambitious dream to venture forth with his tribe to an unfamiliar land and claim it for generations to come. Sarai had a clever plan to provide the son of promise who would become the heir to their future homeland. Together, they both made plans to save their lives and accomplish their shared goals through trickery and half-truths. Their plans and strategy did little to create the outcomes they desired and they ended up fearing for their safety and future. Yet, by the grace of God, the Lord fulfilled His promises through Abraham and Sarah.

How do you cope with the times in your life when it seems like things are not working out the way you planned? It can be very frustrating to make plans for the day or the future that seem to fall apart right before our eyes. I wish I could give you a golden compass that would guide you safely and securely to the future you desire. Although no such compass exists, there is something much better that will point you in the right direction.

Imagine you have something Sarah desperately needed to guide her through the twists and turns of life. You have an opportunity to consult a wise expert who cares deeply for you and is interested in the plans you have made for today, and curious about your hopes for the future. What plans, hopes, or dreams do you want to discuss? You may not have written your plans with pen and paper, but there are probably some ideas you have about your future. What are your concerns, expectations, or fears? What are your hopes and dreams in life? What do you want to accomplish today?

The Lord is waiting for you to seek Him. He loves for us to share our hopes and dreams with Him, and ask for His input, cautions, encouragement, and possible godly alternatives. Ask the Lord for His guidance as you move forward with your life. Picture yourself bringing your charts and timelines, diagrams, drawings, detailed plans, and vague ideas to the Lord. Perhaps you can share a precious dream that you have for the future, that you may not have told anyone else.

The Lord is glad to see you and delighted you would like to know what He thinks. What do you perceive the Lord saying to you? Is there any confirmation? Red flags? A course correction that could revise your plans for the better? How will you respond to the Lord? Will you ask Him to be your daily guide, true north, and Almighty Compass?

Many plans are in a person's heart,
but the advice of the Lord will stand.

Proverbs 19:21 (NASB)

Chapter 2
Serendipity

Joanna's Talent

*A gift opens the way and ushers the giver
into the presence of the great.*

Proverbs 18:16 (NIV)

C huza left home before dawn this morning bound for the estate of Herod Antipas. Manager of an important refurbishment of the living quarters for Antipas and his new wife, Herodias, my husband knows a new wife wants her home free from all reminders of past residents.

Herodias wants a stylishly remodeled home with a special place for her daughter, Salome—a beautiful and seductive young woman. She is clearly her mother's daughter, and I don't trust either one of them. Even so, the renovation is a very challenging and lucrative project. I am very proud of my hard-working husband and pray for his success in pleasing all three: Antipas, Herodias, and Salome. Our future depends on pleasing this powerful familial triad.

Once I see Chuza off for his day, I set about managing the affairs of our home. Our jobs are somewhat similar, since while he works away managing the household of Antipas, I work at home managing ours. Unfortunately, Chuza must endure a household where the politicking inside the house is just as bad, if not worse, than it is outside the house. Thankfully, our home reflects me—calm, comfortable, safe, and secure.

In addition to managing the smooth functioning of my home, I also manage a small project of my own, a creative endeavor that earns me respect and my own income. I have become very good at working with wool fabrics and yarn, creating original patterns and beautiful colors for the prayer shawls that the women in nearby villages purchase for their families and for special occasions. From time to time, I also sell my handiwork to the merchants who pass through town. They in turn sell the prayer shawls in the towns as they go on, along their trade route. I feel happy when I think of how far my handiwork travels. I also feel proud of myself for earning a little financial freedom.

The nomadic caravans brought curious news and odd stories about a prophet traveling in Galilee and preaching about the kingdom of God. This Jewish prophet has attracted the attention of the Pharisees, the people, and even Antipas himself. I heard that when the prophet was warned that Antipas was planning to kill him, he sent a message to Antipas, "Go tell that fox, 'I will keep on driving out demons and healing people today and tomorrow, and on the third day I will reach my goal.'" This man must truly be a prophet. He speaks truth when he calls Antipas a fox! Antipas is clever, unpredictable, and dangerous. It is best to stay on his good side.

About mid-morning I went to the market with a bundle of my prayer shawls. I was very pleased with their luxurious feel

20

and sturdy construction. I felt a little sad to let them go, but I decided that Adonai had a place for my handiwork and a new home with new people who I would never meet. I also knew in my heart that some good would come from the monetary benefit of selling my craft, some good I could not yet imagine.

I delightedly sold the entire bundle of prayer shawls to a quiet, respectful young man at the market. I gave him a fair price for the bunch. Honestly, that a young Jewish man would be interested in more than one prayer shawl surprised me. *He must have special friends or family getting together soon.*

Scanning the noisy market, people crowded around each of the fruit and vegetable carts. Everyone hoped to buy the best the market had to offer for their own family.

Not far away, a shaded plaza offered opportunities for the women to gather and freely trade stories and gossip, each one outdoing the other. One young woman resting in the shade with a large basket of fresh bread beside her caught my attention. *She must be expecting a lot of company.*

Something about her caught and held my gaze. Maybe it was the peaceful expression on her face amid the bustling market and gossiping women that prevented me from looking away. *I must meet her.* I approached her and bent down.

"I am Joanna."

She smiled.

"I am Mary of Magdala, would you like to sit with me?"

I gratefully accepted, thankful for a shady rest, and open to a new friendship.

Our conversation flowed smoothly, as if we had been friends for a long time. I enjoyed her company, and I could have spent all afternoon with her. You can imagine my disappointment when Mary quickly stood to excuse herself.

"I must go now. My basket and I have an appointment!"

"Just one last quick question," I blurted out as she lifted her basket of freshly baked loaves. "Have you heard about the new prophet healing and performing miracles?"

Mary tenderly set the basket back down, smiled warmly, and looked searchingly into my eyes.

"Yes, Joanna, I know of this prophet. He is my rabbi and teacher." She paused, gauging my reaction, then continued.

"He rescued me from seven demons. His name is Jesus, and I will follow him all the days of my life. He is our Messiah. I'm going to meet him and his disciples now. Would you like to come with me?"

I felt a tingle up my spine and a thrill in my heart. What serendipity that the one young woman I met today would be able to introduce me to the prophet everyone is talking about.

Without hesitation I exclaimed, "Yes, let's go!" I excitedly picked up her basket and walked with her to the edge of town. There, I saw a group of people gathered, listening to Jesus' teaching about repentance, forgiveness, and love.

Mary took the basket from me and began distributing loaves among those seated and listening intently to the prophet. As she moved humbly among the people, I noticed how many had prayer shawls over their shoulders. Even Jesus wore a fine, strangely familiar prayer shawl.

Could it be? Is that one my shawls? Indeed, I recognize others as some of the very same prayer shawls I sold just this morning. Then I see the respectful young man who bought them from me. Tears filled my eyes as I saw, for the first time, people I never met who valued my craft.

Drying my eyes, I turned my attention back to Jesus. In a challenging lesson about the kingdom of God, he invited us to repent and turn to God, to love our neighbors, and to pray for our enemies. As he expounded on his open invitation to come into God's kingdom, I felt his gaze fall upon me. My heart burned aflame with the power of his words. In that moment I chose to follow him, to learn from this prophet and teacher, and to honor him with my life. I believed his promise to honor his followers with eternal life.

Deeply moved, my tears flowed freely as I reflected on everything that brought me to this moment: the prayer shawls, the market, Mary, and now seeing Jesus. I was so grateful that Adonai accepted my gifts and talents, and that Jesus accepted me into his kingdom.

"Joanna, dry your eyes."

I looked up to see Mary standing beside me.

"Jesus, this is my friend, Joanna."

Jesus stood beside her.

"Mary tells me you two met this morning, and that you are a very talented artisan and businesswoman."

He used both hands to ever so slightly, but obviously, adjust the prayer shawl draping his shoulders as he smiled at me. *He knows!*

Is it possible to feel both proud and humble at the same time? I hope so because I did. I smiled back and thanked him for sharing his words of life and refreshing my heart and soul.

"The sun will set soon," he announced. "Would you like to join us here again tomorrow?"

"Yes!" I knew that my one brief encounter was not nearly enough. I wanted, no I needed, to know Jesus better every day. As I turned toward home to go and tell Chuza all about my serendipitous day, I suddenly spun around back toward Jesus.

"Teacher, will you accept a gift?"

I reached in my pouch and pulled out the denarii I earned at the market that morning.

"Please, accept this gift to support your ministry sharing about the kingdom of God. I know it isn't much, but I offer it with love and gratitude."

"Of course, Joanna, I accept your gift so freely given. Bless your kindness and generosity. I can assure you that your gift will result in multiplied blessings for the kingdom of God, for you, your husband Chuza, and for your family. Give and it will be given to you."

We just met and he even knows my husband's name? He truly is a prophet!

As I hurry home, I think of Chuza. *I expect we will both have good news to share with one another this evening.* I also reflect on how God's blessing came full circle. I put my heart, energy, and time into crafting the prayer shawls by working freely in the safety of my home. I released my prayer shawls to be used according to their purpose, and they found their way to a group of people who set their hearts to worship God. My earnings then became an opportunity for me to be generous and freely give. In return, I received generous blessings of overwhelming joy for me, my household, and my Chuza—a complete circle of blessings from beginning to end!

Explore

- *Luke 8: 1–3* | Meet Joanna, a follower of Jesus, who contributes from her private means.

- *Luke 8:3* | Chuza is Joanna's husband.

- *Luke 13:31–32* | Jesus sends a message to Herod, who he calls a "fox."

- *Luke 24:10* | Joanna is one of the women at Jesus' tomb early Sunday morning.

- *Matthew 5:44* | Jesus teaches about enemies.

- *John 17:3* | Jesus defines eternal life.

- *2 Corinthians 9:7* | God loves a cheerful giver.

- *Luke 6:38* | Jesus tells us what happens when we give generously.

Reflect

- Can friendship bring a person to meet Jesus? How?

- What opportunities do you have to spend time with Jesus?

- What does serving God mean to you?

- What gifts or talents do you have to offer to God?

- How can a person be humble and proud at the same time?

- In the story, what does Joanna mean when she says that one brief encounter with Jesus is not enough?

Imagine

Picture the moment Joanna meets Jesus, face-to-face. With a twinkle in His eye, He adjusts the prayer shawl on His shoulders to let her know that He recognizes her talent and appreciates her ambition.

Draw near to Jesus now in prayer and imagine yourself face-to-face with the Lord. As He looks into your eyes, what talent does He see in you? What does He appreciate about you? Are there undiscovered skills or special gifts hidden inside you? Receive the recognition and appreciation Jesus has for you and thank Him for noticing! He sees you, and He sees divine potential for your life. Will you embrace the image that Jesus has of you and let your potential become reality through His power and grace and your faith and obedience? Your life, well lived and fully devoted to Jesus, is a gift back to the One who gifted you.

It is more blessed to give than to receive.

Acts 20:35b (NIV)

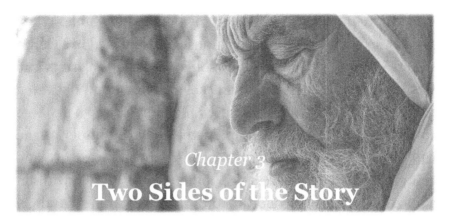

Chapter 3
Two Sides of the Story

At Jesus' Feet

*Do not neglect hospitality to strangers, for by this
some have entertained angels without knowing it.*

Hebrews 13:2 NASB

Side One

O h, how fortunate I am—an influential Pharisee dwelling securely in the Promised Land of my forefathers. You should know, my status is not due to chance but earned by my own hard work. I toiled to steadily ascend the ladder of society to attain our community's most honored position. I became a prominent Pharisee at a young age and am an expert teacher and defender of the Law and our traditions.

I diligently keep my hands clean, and in so doing, avoid soiling my soul with the filth of common people. I thankfully live above the mundane tasks of day-to-day life.

The so-called prophet reportedly traveling throughout our countryside and recently seen here in my own town intrigued me. As part of my religious duty, I decided to meet with him and inquire about his training and knowledge of the Law and traditions which I treasure and passionately defend.

So, I invited Jesus to dine in my home at my table. When I announced my intentions, my household engaged in a frenzy of activity in preparation. They solicited the ripest fruits and freshest vegetables from the market and had them delivered to my door hour by hour while fortunate neighbors contributed delicacies to complete the gourmet dinner menu. Out of religious obligation to rise above the noise, chaos, and confusion I had no other choice but to remove myself, without apology, to the synagogue to pray in quiet and solitude. I worked hard to prepare my mind for the investigation, interview, or whatever this dinner with Jesus turned out to be.

I expected the man at the twelfth hour—6 p.m. Though he arrived late, he offered no apology for disrespecting me. Even so, I promptly directed him to my table where the rest of my honored guests were already reclining while waiting for him to arrive.

Suddenly, without warning, and without my permission, a well-known sinner slipped into our gathering. Before I could expel her, she knelt behind Jesus. Out of curiosity, I waited to see what the unclean intruder would do next. I heard sobbing, and realized she was crying, weeping giant tears all over the feet of my guest. She then took her long, dark hair and used it like a towel to wipe his feet. Then she kissed each foot and began anointing them with perfumed oil from a valuable alabaster vial she apparently brought with her.

As she continued her uninvited, humiliating performance, I increasingly felt embarrassed and dishonored in my own home. I and my guests watched Jesus just sit there and take it. *If this man is really a prophet, would he not most certainly know what sort of woman this is? Yet, he allows this sinner to keep touching him!*

I knew of the unholy character and unrighteousness of the woman long before she dared enter my home. I did not previously know Jesus but could now see clearly what kind of man he was, no matter his claims.

A voice broke the uncomfortable silence of my guests and the now murmured sobs of the obnoxious sinner and her newest object of affection.

"Simon," Jesus announced, "I have something to say to you."

"Speak." I was in no good mood.

Jesus posed a riddle about a lender and two debtors who could not repay their debts. One owed a small debt, and the other a large one, yet the lender forgave them both.

"Simon, which debtor would love the lender more?"

The answer is so obvious. Is this a trap? Or maybe he's testing me as I am testing him.

"The one forgiven the most would love more."

Jesus motioned toward the intruder.

"Simon, do you see this woman?"

How could I not? We all saw her and heard her. She was still kneeling, weeping, disgustingly touching this man in MY house, and anointing his feet with oil and wiping it with her hair. *Yes, we all see her and you allowing her to touch you!*

"When I entered your house, you did not provide water to wash my feet, nor did you greet me with a kiss, nor did you anoint my head with oil."

Technically true, but you were late, and rude, and...

"This woman washed my feet with her tears and wiped them with her hair; she has kissed my feet and anointed them with perfumed oil. I tell you Simon, her sins, which are many, are forgiven."

29

He turned to the woman and spoke to her, "Your sins are forgiven."

He certainly speaks with authority. But we all know that only God can forgive sin.

"Your faith has saved you, go in peace."

As she departed, Jesus scanned my table of guests and returned his gaze to me.

"Those who are forgiven little love little, and those who are forgiven much love much."

Boom! The impact of this truth cut straight to the heart. I was surprised, maybe all of us were, because these words were true and right. Those who are forgiven the most would love the most in return.

As a practicing Pharisee, I religiously kept all the required rules and traditions. My nearly perfect behavior meant that I didn't need forgiveness, except perhaps for unintentional, unknown sins. *Is Jesus insinuating that my love for God is somehow less since I need less forgiveness, if any? Does one have to sin greatly to experience great love for God?* These thoughts seemed confusing.

Weeks later, as Jesus continued publicly teaching and preaching, he outright condemned people who expressed pious confidence in their own self-righteousness and who looked down on people they considered inferior. Maybe he wasn't calling me out by name, but it seemed personal to me.

So, I felt compelled to go, listen, and evaluate Jesus' public teaching. I went to the market, which was packed, and easily slipped into the crowd unnoticed. I cautiously blended in with people gathered near Jesus. I leaned in and listened closely. Per his apparent custom, he was telling a parable—a simple story with a spiritual truth tucked inside.

"Two men went up to the temple to pray, one a Pharisee and the other a tax collector. The Pharisee stood by himself and prayed: 'God, I thank you that I am not like other people—robbers, evildoers, adulterers—or even like this tax collector. I fast twice a week and give a tenth of all I get.' But the tax collector stood at a distance. He would not even look up to heaven, but beat his breast and said, 'God, have mercy on me, a sinner.'"

Jesus paused and scanned the crowd.

"I tell you that the tax collector, rather than the Pharisee, went home justified before God."

His gaze passed in my direction without pause. *Maybe he saw me. Maybe not.*

"For all those who exalt themselves will be humbled, and those who humble themselves will be exalted."

His words once again pierced my protective veil. But this time, instead of dismissing the point, I felt a stinging stab of self-awareness. *Ouch! In his story, I would have been the Pharisee. Jesus was talking about me—I am the Pharisee!*

After the disastrous dinner at my home, my influential friends shunned me for inviting Jesus and allowing the unclean, uninvited, weeping woman to wash his feet publicly. While they judged me and we judged Jesus and the woman, she acted with humility. I now clearly saw our arrogance.

As I continued to listen to Jesus warn about the dangers of self-righteousness and considered his ways, I realized I wanted to know him, and find out more about forgiveness, humble living, and loving God. I not only wanted to be a Pharisee, but I also wanted to be a good Pharisee. *I want to go home justified before God. Have mercy on me, a sinner!*

Explore

- *Luke 7:36–50* | There is a story within Pharisee Simon's dinner story. Whose story is it?

- *Luke 7:42* | DEBT FORGIVENESS: Everyone needs it!

- *Luke 18:9–14* (NIV) | Jesus may have had someone like Simon the Pharisee in mind.

Side Two

People talk. They talk a lot about me, and out of the same mouth they talk about Jesus. They talk about my so-called sinful life, and they talk about Jesus and his holy life. For a change, I've been listening to Jesus, even if only from a distance. He doesn't talk like others talk.

People watch. They watch my every move to make sure every misstep and each sin is noted and documented. They watch Jesus, too, looking for an opportunity to accuse him also. I've been watching Jesus, too, even if only from a distance. He doesn't act like others act.

I was thrilled when I heard Jesus accepted an invitation as an honored guest in the home of a local Pharisee, Simon. I knew very well how to get to Simon's house, and I knew this might be my best opportunity to get close to Jesus. His words of love and forgiveness pierced my heart when I heard him speak to the crowd. His acts of compassion touched my soul and brought me to tears when I saw him with people in the street. I knew I needed Jesus, I needed love and forgiveness, and I needed a new life full of holiness, not sinfulness. Jesus was my only hope for a fresh start and a new life.

I carefully navigated the streets to Simon's home that evening. I stood mostly unnoticed among the gathering crowd, since everyone was distracted watching for Jesus. I stationed myself near the courtyard entry where I hoped to intercept the Teacher with a humble bow and quick moment of privacy.

However, when Jesus arrived late, Simon hastened his entry and whisked him inside to the seat of honor prepared for him at the table. Dinner began with Simon presiding as master of ceremonies. Amidst the bustle, I was able to slip into the dining room. I was not to be deterred, not now, and not this close!

I approached Jesus quietly and from behind, hoping not to call attention to myself. However, as I knelt beside him, I began to weep. I ached for one small gesture of forgiveness for me, personally, just as I saw many times before when he touched others. If only Jesus would speak to me and help me. I needed him more than breath itself.

Lost in the moment, I suddenly realized my tears were staining the layer of dust accumulated on his feet during his journey to Simon's home. Without really thinking about it, I grabbed my hair and began wiping the tears and dirt away. Normally, a host would have arranged for feet washing prior to entry, but Jesus' feet were still dirty, so I cleaned them with the things I had available, my tears and my hair.

Overwhelmed with unfathomable emotion, I kissed his feet and then anointed them with perfumed oil from an alabaster vial that I carried in my tunic. In my mind, the world faded away and no one and nothing else existed except me bowing at the feet of Jesus.

A distant voice sounded, and my ears tuned to the familiar warm sound of Jesus speaking.

"Simon," Jesus announced, "I have something to say to you."

"Speak." Simon seemed in no good mood.

Jesus posed a riddle about a lender and two debtors who could not repay their debts. One owed a small debt, and the other a large one, yet the lender forgave them both.

"Simon, which debtor would love the lender more?"

The answer is so obvious. Is this a trap? Or maybe he's testing Simon as other Pharisees test him.

"The one forgiven the most would love more."

Jesus motioned toward me.

"Simon, do you see this woman?"

I was suddenly overcome by a bolt of fear that shot through my body like lightening. Jesus was calling attention to me in front of everyone.

"When I entered your house, you did not provide water to wash my feet, nor did you greet me with a kiss, nor did you anoint my head with oil. This woman washed my feet with her tears and wiped them with her hair; she has kissed my feet and anointed them with perfumed oil. I tell you Simon, her sins, which are many, are forgiven."

Then Jesus turned to me with love in eyes and spoke tenderly, but with unquestionable authority, "Your sins are forgiven."

My fear evaporated instantaneously. I felt a warm sense of love and forgiveness. Jesus saw me, knew my heart, perceived my deep faith in him, and my deep need. Jesus spoke to me, to me! He extended compassion on me, the lowest of low. His words and his actions were exactly what I had heard and seen from him over the time I followed him.

As I stood to depart, Jesus returned his gaze to Simon and his table guests.

"Those who are forgiven little love little," Jesus told them. "And those who are forgiven much love much."

Boom! The impact of this truth cut straight to the heart. I was surprised, maybe all of us were, because these words were true and right. Those who are forgiven the most would love the most in return. I was then and there forgiven for so much; my heart was filled with love.

Jesus turned and spoke to me again.

"Your faith has saved you, go in peace."

Peace.

Peace?

Peace! I felt it. It was strange and foreign, but lovely.

After that, I began to watch. I watched for the lowly and humble of heart. I began to talk to people, too, and tell them about Jesus and how his love and forgiveness brought me peace in this life, along with hope for peace in the life beyond.

I also felt compelled to go and continue listening to Jesus when he taught in public. When I heard he was teaching at the market one day, I went. It was packed, and I easily slipped into the crowd unnoticed. I cautiously blended in with people gathered near Jesus. I leaned in and listened closely. Per his custom, he was telling a parable—a simple story with a spiritual truth tucked inside.

"Two men went up to the temple to pray, one a Pharisee and the other a tax collector. The Pharisee stood by himself and prayed: 'God, I thank you that I am not like other people— robbers, evildoers, adulterers—or even like this tax collector. I fast twice a week and give a tenth of all I get.' But the tax collector stood at a distance. He would not even look up to heaven, but beat his breast and said, 'God, have mercy on me, a sinner.'"

Jesus paused and scanned the crowd.

"I tell you that the tax collector, rather than the Pharisee, went home justified before God."

His gaze passed in my direction without pause. *Maybe he saw me. Maybe not. I would love to tell him about the many wonderful things that have happened in my life since the night he forgave me at Simon's house!*

"For all those who exalt themselves will be humbled, and those who humble themselves will be exalted."

I identified with the one who felt unworthy. Yet, as in the parable, Jesus justified me and offered me God's love and forgiveness. I felt deep gratitude for his act of generosity and freedom from a debt too great to be repaid. I smiled and looked up for Jesus but, in doing so, noticed Simon the Pharisee standing right in front of me.

I felt a prick of panic. *I wonder if he recognizes me?*

Simon looked up. I stood there frozen, not sure what to say or do.

"Hello. What is your name?"

"Lily," I answered hesitantly.

"Like the flower?"

"Yes."

He smiled. "Well, Lily, I am about to invite our Jesus to dinner in my home again. Would you be so kind as to join us?"

I was speechless. *In what world would a Pharisee invite me to join him in his home. For dinner. Me? And with Jesus?*

Simon continued.

"You surprised me, Lily. You honored Jesus in my home even as I failed to honor him myself as his host. You modeled

36

the type of humility that God approves, and I learned a great lesson from you through Jesus. I'm still learning, but I know that I owe you a great debt of gratitude. I hope you will join us as my guest. Together, we will honor Jesus as our Redeemer, Lord, and Savior."

Explore

- *James 3:10* (NIV) | GOSSIP: How to talk out of both sides of your mouth.

- *Luke 7:36* | The invited dinner guest.

- *Luke 7:37* | The uninvited dinner guest.

- *Luke 18:9–14* | The Parable of the Pharisee hits home.

Reflect

- How did Simon become so religious that he seems of little earthly good to his household?

- What does the humble gesture of Lily tell you about her religion?

- Simon treasured the Law, tradition, and status. Lily treasured forgiveness and Jesus. What do you treasure?

- Simon and Lily responded differently to Jesus' statement: "Those who are forgiven little love little, and those who are forgiven much love much." How do you respond?

- How does a canceled debt compare to forgiveness?

- Why did Simon the Pharisee have a change of heart?

- How did Simon show his changed heart?

- Who got a second chance in the story?

- How are the stories different? How are they similar?

Imagine

Picture yourself in the home of Simon the Pharisee in a great room with a large center table. A feast fit for a king is spread out in front of you and Simon is presiding. Each place at the table is occupied by a very important person. One open spot awaits the guest of honor. After Jesus is seated, a disreputable woman enters and humbly kneels behind him at his feet. She is crying and appears to be seeking and extremely sorry.

Do you feel comfortable with Jesus in the room? Who are you at the table? A curious on-looker? A skeptic? A believer? Simon the Pharisee? The woman?

Pause to consider how you relate to Jesus. No one is perfect like God. We all fall short of His holiness. We mess up sooner or later. Tell Jesus, if you can, where you need His forgiveness today. Take as much time as you need. Jesus sees you, He hears your heart, don't hold back. Then listen for Jesus' voice telling you that your faith in Him has saved you. You are forgiven. Go in peace.

If we confess our sins, he is faithful and just and will forgive us our sins and purify us from all unrighteousness.

1 John 1:9 (NIV)

Chapter 4
God Is Listening

Miriam's Mouth

*Those who guard their mouths and their tongues
keep themselves from calamity.*

Proverbs 21:23 (NIV)

T he Lord said to me, Moses, and Aaron, "You three. Come out to the tent of meeting."

At that moment, we three siblings and venerated leaders of the freed Jewish slaves felt like little children "invited" out to the woodshed for a "talk" with dad. Together, we walked tentatively toward the tent—God's house and where serious, truthful conversations occurred.

I wondered, *What did little brother Moses do now?* I was used to playing the role of the more mature, resourceful, and watchful older sister.

Aaron was probably wondering what me or Moses did to initiate this summoning. Maybe he thought that perhaps God had a course correction for Miriam or Moses.

Moses was probably praying as we approached the holy place where he regularly communed with God. He does that.

It never crossed my mind that perhaps I was in trouble. Since early in life, I have shown myself to be a leader, and shrewd under pressure. As a child, I helped rescue Moses from fairly certain death. In obedience to Pharaoh's command to throw all male Hebrew children in the Nile River, momma put Moses in the reeds by the edge of the river, albeit in a basket coated with tar and pitch so it that just so happened to float! But she technically obeyed the law.

I watched my little brother carefully from a distance. When Pharaoh's daughter came down to the river to bathe, one of her attendants found the basket and took it to her. Right as she opened it and realized it was one the Hebrew children, I quickly intervened with a plan that positioned our own mother as Moses' caretaker and nurse. Not only that, but Pharoah's daughter also paid momma to take care of him! Since then, I have received a lot of compliments for my courage and cleverness.

After our exodus from Egypt, I helped lead our women in celebratory song and dance and served as an inspirational and creative worship leader. I think my song has been quite an encouragement to our people since we traveled and often sang together, "Sing to the Lord for He is highly exalted."

I have also served as Israel's first female prophet, or prophetess. I suppose my pedigree and connection to Moses and Aaron helped bolster my reputation since I have heard of young girls who have said, "When I grow up, I want to be like Miriam!" And yet, all that glitters is not gold.

Prior to this little invitation to meet with the Lord, I bad-mouthed Moses. In retrospect, I envied the immense respect people have for Moses and the special way that only he gets to communicate with God "face-to-face." I longed for that same degree of respect for me, as well as for Aaron. I mean, after all, we thought we deserved at least that much. We are the older siblings! What makes Moses so special anyway?

I remember talking with Aaron and us asking ourselves, "Has the Lord indeed spoken only through Moses? Has He not spoken through us as well?" I suppose other people heard us talking and soon gossip spread like wildfire and everyone in the camp heard about our little sibling spat.

Initially, I think the trouble started because I took issue with Moses' wife. Like many older sisters, I felt protective of my little brother, even if he was all grown up. Maybe I felt possessive of Moses and jealous of the attention he gave her, an outsider. We were three long before she ever showed up. So, I lashed out, questioned Moses' position, decision-making and wisdom, and threw some serious shade on God's chosen. Unfortunately, I was not clever enough to realize that in speaking out against Moses, I was speaking out against God.

As the gossip spread, God heard it too! Hence, the summoning. After we arrived at the tent of meeting, the Lord came and appeared in the doorway in a pillar of cloud. He called me and Aaron to step forward and charged us to listen.

"When there is a prophet among you, I, the Lord, reveal myself to them in visions, I speak to them in dreams."

We nodded. Yes, we recognized this as two of the ways God communicates with his prophets.

"But this is not true of my servant Moses, with him I speak face to face, clearly and not in riddles. Why then were you not afraid to speak against my servant Moses?"

I'll admit, I felt a crushing pang in the pit of my stomach. I also felt tingly all over—God was calling me out, and I felt it. I not only disrespected our unique leader, I disrespected God.

The Lord was so angry with us that He withdrew from us. One moment, we were suffering His righteous indignation and wrath due to our petty jealousy, pride, and sibling rivalry, and the next moment the Lord was gone.

Aaron noticed me first. As he recoiled in horror, we all three realized that I was covered in leprosy, a highly contagious and deadly skin disease. My skin was white as snow. It was as if the poisonous thoughts eating away inside my heart, mind, and soul had escaped outward and enveloped my body like a shroud of death.

Aaron cried out, "Please, Moses, I ask you not to hold against us the sin we have so foolishly committed. Do not let her be like a stillborn infant coming from its mother's womb with its flesh half eaten away."

His outcry owned it all: our envy, slander, and pride. I think maybe he recognized that our lifelong three was about to become two without divine intervention. I was terrified.

Moses immediately cried out, "Please God, heal her!"

Then, we waited.

The Lord answered Moses, "Let her be shut out of the camp for seven days; after that, she can be brought back in." This matched several of our rules about what to do when people had a skin disease or had touched a dead body. Maybe it meant I would be healed during that time, but I wasn't completely sure.

I spent the next week confined to a tent, by myself, alone—apart from my family and our people; isolated for seven long days and nights. Thankfully, the entire camp waited all week for me to finish my punishment and quarantine before they moved on to the next stop in our long journey.

I realized some things that week. One, it is hard to talk when no one is listening. For seven unending days, I was surrounded by no one. No one to talk to, no one to listen, but God. So, I talked to Him. I prayed. As I opened my heart and revealed my soul, I realized the Lord listens, all the time.

Two, I learned to really listen. I heard the distant sounds of our people in their camps, but mostly listened to the silence. I got better at listening. I heard the sound of forgiveness, felt peace, and realized along the way that I was not alone.

As my heart and soul reconciled with God, I experienced peace and healing. When I emerged after seven long days and nights in the tent, everyone could see that my body was completely restored. What they could not immediately see was the restoration of my soul.

My family—especially Aaron and Moses—and friends joyfully welcomed me back home. I was restored to them, our people, and my leadership position. But I was not the same woman who walked out to the tent with Aaron and Moses to meet with the Lord a week earlier.

I suppose my life reveals the consequences of sin AND the blessing of undeserved forgiveness and grace. As we reunited, we three siblings were stronger because of what we went through together. Aaron and I much more clearly understood Moses' unique calling, our privilege to serve along with him each in our respective roles, the importance of integrity, the need to avoid slander and subversion, and our calling as representatives serving God on behalf of the people. We soon discovered that the road ahead would not be easy, nor nearly as short as we expected. But, God always proved a faithful Father, even if sometimes we were not faithful to Him. It was His love that called to us when He called us to account.

Explore

- *Numbers 12:1–16* | The seeds of jealousy are planted. God is not happy about it.

- *Exodus 15:21* | Miriam's Song of Praise.

- *Numbers 1:18* (KJV) | The people "declared their pedigrees."

- *Exodus 33:11* (NIV) | The LORD spoke to Moses face to face.

- *Numbers 12:14* (NASB) | IRONIC: Miriam, shut out of the camp, was shut up for a time!

Reflect

- How do you think Miriam felt outside the camp for seven days?

- What do you do when you feel alone?

- How might alone time be good for you?

- Do you agree with Miriam that God is always listening?

- If God is listening, is that good news, bad news, or maybe both?

Imagine

What would it feel like to be isolated, alone in a tent out in the wilderness? It's easy to imagine that the only sound you might hear is the wind, or perhaps the beating of your own heart. Do you hear it? Silence can be very loud!

Maybe you are not alone. You gradually sense a Presence that feels like a cloud of mist filling your tent. It is the Lord. He is there with you, ready to listen.

Tell the Lord what is on your mind. Pour out your heart. Tell Him your fears, doubts, questions, and needs both great and small. Do you have something to celebrate? Thank Him and share your joys as well as your concerns. He will stay with you until you finish. There is no rush. He has all the time in the world.

When you run out of words, listen. Does the Lord have something to say to you? He loves to forgive when we repent, encourage us when we feel doubtful, strengthen us when we feel weak, and join us in celebrating our victories.

He hears prayers. He hears your prayers. He is your number one Fan and loves you more deeply than you could ever imagine.

As you leave your tent, think about how you feel after spending time alone with God. Is anything different? Are you different?

You will make known to me the way of life;
in Your presence is fullness of joy;
in Your right hand there are pleasures forever.

Psalm 16:11 (NASB)

Chapter 5
I Believe

Mary of Bethany's Offering

Do not forget to do good and to share with others,
for with such sacrifices God is pleased.

Hebrews 13:16 (NIV)

My heart pounds excitedly as we prepare to enjoy dinner in honor of Jesus in Simon the Leper's home. I wish we could give him a new name, like "Simon-the-man-who-used-to-have-leprosy-but-doesn't-anymore-because-Jesus-healed-him." Of course, that is too long, so we just keep calling him Simon the Leper and everyone knows who we mean.

We have much to celebrate—the miracle and blessing of Simon's healing, as well as the astounding miracle of my brother, Lazarus. Following his sickness and death, we sadly washed, anointed, and wrapped his body and buried him in our family tomb. Four days later, Jesus arrived, way too late to do anything about it, or so we thought. When he finally showed up, Jesus asked us to roll the stone away. But, my sister Martha, who totally trusts Jesus, tried to deter him.

"Lord, by this time, there is a bad odor, since he has been in there four days."

But Jesus insisted, reminded her that if she believed she would see the glory of God, and he prayed. Then he stood at the tomb entrance and called out Lazarus' name. It was strange. We assumed the dead were dead, and deaf!

But there he was, shouting into the dark void. *If Jesus wanted to talk to my brother, he could have showed up days ago and maybe we wouldn't be in this situation...*

"Lazarus! Come forth!"

And he did. We could hardly believe it! Our undoubtedly-four-days-dead-brother awoke from the sleep of death and walked out of the tomb. When we unwrapped him, he was amazingly alive, all healed from his sickness, and hungry!

We certainly experienced the glory of God as Jesus vividly demonstrated his power over life and death by restoring our brother. Even though we don't completely understand it, we are certain Jesus is the Messiah, the Chosen One for whom our people have longed for centuries.

So, you can understand the sense of joyful celebration that permeates our hearts and minds. Jesus is coming to dinner tonight, and today everything feels golden.

As the sun sets, a light breeze brings us some relief from the heat of the day. We gather expectantly at Simon's, and Jesus is with us.

With increasing darkness, the lamplight more brightly illuminates many happy faces around the table. Simon beams with thankfulness for his friends and family enjoying one another's company. Martha and Lazarus glow as they sit close, savoring the opportunity to share another meal. Disciples cheerily share a few silly stories about themselves and their ministry travels. Jesus' presence fills the room with a sense of holiness that touches all who are present.

I feel it. We are all here and filled with joy because of him, even though he is probably tired from all the hustle and bustle of teaching and healing and dealing with crowds filled with both friend and foe. I want to minister to him in some way.

I remember the jar of nard, a fragrant and expensive perfumed oil our family set aside for a special occasion. In fact, Martha and I used similar oils when we anointed Lazarus for his burial. I rise quietly but purposefully from the table, hurry home to retrieve the jar, return, and make my way to Jesus. He sees me and accepts me graciously as I generously pour oil on his head.

Jesus seems deeply reflective, perhaps even burdened, and simultaneously comforted by my actions. I use the remaining oil in the jar to anoint his feet, then wipe his feet with my hair. The aroma of the herb-infused oil rises like a prayer and fills the room, aromatically depicting the overwhelming sense of love I have for Jesus in my heart.

My brother, sister, and I are good friends with Jesus— more like family, really. I cannot even express the depth of my wonder and appreciation for him bringing our brother back to life. However, I am also sorry for my despairing words to Jesus upon his arrival after the death of Lazarus, "Lord, if You had been here my brother would not have died."

I believed that wholeheartedly. However, my faith and respect included resentment that Jesus was not with us when Lazarus was sick and when we believed he would most be able to help our brother, his good friend. At the time, we considered death's door a one-way threshold.

As I tie my hair back up into a knot, Judas Iscariot speaks loudly and accusingly, "Why didn't you sell this perfumed oil and give the money to the poor?"

He serves as treasurer of the disciples and takes financial matters quite seriously. His manner startles me, and suddenly I wonder if my actions were somehow selfish. John starts to question Judas if he is worried about losing a commission when Jesus interrupts.

"Leave her alone." He stares at Judas. "It was intended that Mary would set this nard aside for my burial, rather than for you to sell it for a profit."

I look down at the jar in my hands.

His burial? The jar is empty, except for the lingering remnants on my hands, in mine and Jesus' hair, and on his feet. No, there is no oil left to use for Jesus' burial.

But Jesus clearly isn't dead. Hasn't he raised Lazarus who is just as alive as Jesus. If he could raise my brother to life, why would Jesus die? No, I decide, Jesus must live as surely as my brother Lazarus now lives!

After a long, emotional evening, I return home. Thoughts about the future and difficult questions swirl around in my mind.

Jesus leaves Bethany the next day and continues to Jerusalem for Passover. Many Jews have heard of Jesus and his miracles and have been waiting to welcome him into the capital city. They greet him with waving palm branches and the proclamation, "Hosanna! Blessed is he who comes in the name of the Lord. Blessed is the king of Israel."

Martha and I stay behind with Lazarus. Because people are sharing the news about Jesus raising our brother from the dead, the ruling Sadducees are threatening to kill Lazarus. The miracle is causing many Jews to turn to Jesus, and the Sadducees see Lazarus as a threat to their power. Since they do not even believe in resurrection, they are angry!

Jesus is in danger, too. The Sadducees had already been threatening his life; my brother's miracle just increased the fervor of their hatred. I so wish they would just believe in him, yet my heart breaks knowing that both Pharisees and Sadducees cannot accept that Jesus could be the Messiah!

As Jesus rode toward Jerusalem, I watched him as long as I could. *If the nard was reserved for his burial, how could that be, since no oil is left? Also, if he was really facing death, surely Jesus would not be riding into Jerusalem. As smart and sneaky as they were, the Sadducees, Pharisees and Romans were no match for the authority and power of Jesus.*

Yet, his words hung in the air. "Only believe," he told me. "I am the resurrection and the life. The one who believes in me will live, even though they die." We believed and we saw what happened with Lazarus. I'm still not sure I understand, but I do know this: I believe in Jesus.

Explore

- *John 11:1–44* | Mary, Martha, Lazarus, and Simon the Leper all live in Bethany.

- *Mark 14:3–9* | Jesus' head is anointed with pure nard at Simon the Leper's home.

- *Matthew 26:6–7* | Jesus' head is anointed with perfume at Simon the Leper's home.

- *John 12:1–8* | Jesus' feet are anointed with a pint of nard at a home in Bethany.

- *Mark 14:8* | HARMONIZING THE GOSPELS: Mark, Matthew, and John tell us this story. Jesus pulls all three versions of the event together when he says that Mary anointed his "body" for burial.

- *John 12:6* | Judas loses the commission on the sale of the nard.

- *John 12:10–13* | GUILT BY ASSOCIATION: Lazarus is a wanted man.

- *John 11:25* | Jesus promises eternal life to all who believe in Him.

Reflect

- Do you celebrate the presence of Jesus in your life?

- How do you respond if the circumstances of life challenge your beliefs?

- Do you believe Jesus' statement that if you believe in him, you will live forever?

Imagine

How do you feel when life doesn't make sense? Do unwelcome doubts and unanswered questions drift across your mind, and sometimes settle into your thoughts? Picture those doubts and questions floating somewhere above you now. Perhaps it looks like there is a flock of noisy crows circling overhead. Maybe there is just one persistent doubt that resembles a dark rain cloud that's ready to burst. Now is a good time to talk with Jesus. Questions don't scare Him. Tell Him what lingers on your mind. Let Him know what you don't understand about life, about yourself, or about Him. Talking with Jesus helps. Questions are allowed, always. Ask away! It will do you good to honestly share your concerns with Jesus. He already knows your secret thoughts, He loves you deeply, and He longs for you to trust Him with your heart and thoughts.

What if, after talking with Jesus, your concerns are still unsettled? Do you need all your questions to be answered to believe in Jesus? Or do you need just enough belief in Jesus that allows some of your questions to go unanswered, for now? Jesus understands that sometimes it's hard to believe. Tell Him how hard it is to keep on believing when you don't understand. Ask Jesus to help you keep believing even if your questions go unanswered, for now. Jesus wants you to remember that if you believe in Him you will live, now and in eternity.

I do believe; help me overcome my unbelief.

Mark 9:24 (NIV)

53

Chapter 6

Judgment Day

Caught in the Act

Do not follow the crowd in doing wrong...
do not pervert justice by siding with the crowd.

Exodus 23:2a and c (NIV)

A panicked voice pierced the stillness of the predawn
hour. The loyal friend's urgent knocking shook the
Pharisee's entire household.

"Come quickly, it's your daughter!"

"What?"

"Hurry! She's in the temple courtyard."

As word spread about a woman caught in the act of
adultery, a mob of Pharisees and curious onlookers began
gathering to stone her. However, some suggested taking her
to Jesus, the Teacher, to pronounce her sentence and lead the
execution. The friend ran to notify her father as members of
the mob drug her toward the courtyard to find Jesus and let
her face the public consequences of her private life.

Groggy and disheveled, the Pharisee threw his cloak over
his shoulder and stumbled through the door while his mind
struggled to grasp the scene his friend described. *Is it really*

my precious daughter, whom I have not seen or spoken to for some time, at the center of a crowd at our temple, publicly exposed, and waiting for judgment?

He loved her and grieved over the struggles she faced trying to live up to the expectations people had for the daughter of a Pharisee. She rebelled against the Law of Moses and abandoned herself to a lifestyle that threw impossible expectations into the trash. She embraced her own path yet seemingly found even less happiness in her "freedom."

As a Pharisee, her father recoiled in disgust and shame over his daughter's lifestyle. His religious devotion required separation from anything and anyone liable to soil his purity of devotion to God or interfere with his compliance with the Law of Moses. His love for God, he believed, compelled him to separate himself even from his own daughter to avoid his own separation from God.

Rushing and pushing through the streets, the Pharisee remembered seeing Jesus teaching at the temple just two days earlier. The Teacher spoke to a crowd of ordinary people as he and other Pharisees watched from the edge.

"Stop judging by mere appearances," Jesus warned, "but instead judge correctly."

Although speaking to the crowd, the Pharisees perceived Jesus' words as a personal rebuke. They were indignant that this so-called "Teacher" dared reprove them publicly. Yet now his own wandering daughter was about to face this same Jesus and, as a Pharisee, her father would be called to join Jesus in approving of her judgment according to the Law.

This is all so overwhelming! He had tried so hard to compartmentalize his world by putting his devotion to God and the Law of Moses in one box, and his family in another.

But the boxes were difficult to keep separate. Angst filled his waking thoughts and worrisome dreams filled many fitful nights. The words of the Prophet Micah constantly weighed heavy on his heart and perplexed his mind:

"He has shown you, O man, what is good; And what does the Lord require of you? But to do justly, to love mercy, and to walk humbly with your God."

Unable to reconcile justice and mercy when it came to his daughter, he gave up in his own way, too. He committed to follow the righteous and approved path of judgment. And yet, somehow, his choice filled him with sadness.

Arriving at the temple, now fully awake, he remembered again just how angry he and other Pharisees felt when Jesus rebuked them. A few suggested setting a trap for the upstart rabbi, enjoining a conundrum to extract their revenge. Now, he sickeningly realized his very own daughter might be the honey his fellow Pharisees would use to trap the annoying fly.

As he advanced through the throbbing crowd, he glimpsed his terrified daughter. She lay awkwardly on the ground surrounded by some of his Pharisee friends, fellow lovers of God, and followers of the Law of Moses. He also saw Jesus standing within their circle, almost hovering over his daughter. He felt like someone stabbed him with two swords, one in the front and one in the back.

"Teacher," shouted one of his fellow Pharisees. "This woman has been caught in the very act of adultery."

The crowd hushed. These were lurid allegations. Maybe more details were forthcoming.

Another Pharisee announced loudly, "In the Law, Moses commanded us to stone such women; what do you say?"

The trap was set, and his daughter was the bait. If Jesus agreed with the law of Moses to please the Pharisees, this would violate Roman law that prevented Jews from exercising capital punishment. But, if Jesus disagreed with Jewish Law, he would disqualify himself from consideration as a righteous and obedient teacher. Oh, how his fellow Pharisees grinned with pride at their clever trap positing an impossible theological and legal conundrum for Jesus. They shamelessly sought to advance their own reputation, increase their authority, and publicly mock this upstart rabbi. Yet, in their rush to judgement, they foolishly ignored a wise admonition from the Book of Proverbs, "Pride goes before destruction."

In response to their challenge, Jesus unexpectedly knelt in front of his daughter, tapped his finger on the ground, and began moving it, writing something in the dust. One by one, the Pharisees curiously shifted their gazes from Jesus and her to the letters taking shape on the ground. Not everyone could see, but the arrogant demeanor of those closest to Jesus and able to read the words seemed to shift toward sour grimaces of discomfort.

What message is this? The judgment of his daughter written in fulfillment of Jeremiah's words, "Those who turn away from you, God, will be written in the dust"? Or names, wait, multiple names of...of Pharisees? What kind of list is Jesus writing? He couldn't quite make it out.

The waves of blind rage and demands that Jesus quit delaying and issue his judgement rippled away from the center toward the edges of the crowd. The crowd grew silent.

Jesus stood and slowly scanned the angry faces of the surrounding Pharisees. He looked at them, gazed deeply into their eyes, and stepped aside from the weeping bait and prey.

"He who is without sin among you," he motioned underhandedly to the crowd and then pointed to the woman, "let him be the first to throw a stone at her."

Then he bent and continued writing in the dusty ground. He didn't even bother to look up and emanated a calm sense of unusual nonchalance.

Thump.

The sound of a stone's impact startled her father.

Thump. Thump.

But these were not loud impacts from stones hurled with might and fury, but soft thuds.

Several Pharisees closest to the center of the crowd turned outward and began to filter their way through the crowd, away from Jesus and the Pharisee's daughter.

"Judge correctly," Jesus taught as many of these same Pharisees listened days earlier. They now found themselves in a position to judge themselves according to the Law of Moses.

The desperate woman saw her father's face among the crowd. She hoped he might somehow rescue her from the sentence of death by speaking up on her behalf. Yet, when their eyes met, he quickly dropped his gaze, and they both saw the rock in his hand.

When did I pick up a rock?

Startled, he dropped the stone. He then turned away from his daughter, which was tragically normal. But this instance seemed less familiar. He did not seem as proud and arrogant, but seemingly broken and sad, burdened by an invisible heavy weight on his soul. Faced with the conviction of his own guilt, he turned away from the cauldron of conviction filled with the hateful brew cooked up by his friends. He would not eat today.

Quietly, as more and more older Pharisees dropped their stones and walked away, younger ones followed suit, and the entire crowd eventually dispersed.

Jesus turned and asked, "Woman, where are they? Did no one condemn you?"

"No one, Lord," she cautiously replied.

"Then, neither do I condemn you. Go, and sin no more."

She stared at Jesus in disbelief. *Is this forgiveness? I am not condemned to die? I am free? I am free. I am free!*

Her father always taught that only God could forgive sin. And yet here was this man, Jesus, forgiving her, and no one, not even her father, remained to protest his judgment.

In that private and sacred moment, she recognized her savior as Lord and Messiah. She felt the grace of God in her soul and through Jesus found forgiveness and true freedom.

She suddenly felt a sense of urgency. She sensed the glimmer of a narrow path forward to make things right with her father and quickly rose and turned her steps toward home. She knew the way, even though the outcome of these steps appeared uncertain.

What will my father do? Will he even talk to me when I arrive? Will he continue to harshly judge and condemn me? Will he coldly withdraw and expel me from his presence?

She felt restored to God but wondered if restoration with her father was possible. Though doubts threatened to redirect her steps, hope proved stronger and propelled her forward.

As she entered the courtyard, her father stood alone in the center. He appeared deeply focused in prayer, his face turned toward the ground, hands open, and palms lifted toward heaven. Streams of tears tracked through the film of dust that layered his face. She paused at the door, weeping quietly.

But not quietly enough. He heard a sound and turned to see her timidly standing at the door. Without reservation, he extended his arms and she rushed forward. They grasped each other for a long time before either spoke. When they did, they both confessed their own arrogance, condemnations of each other, and blindness to their own shortcomings, faults, and sins. They now judged correctly, beginning with themselves, as Jesus had challenged.

The Pharisee gently wiped his daughter's eyes, and then his own. Lost among misguided longing and seeking to do justice and love mercy at the same time, he now understood that Moses' Law brought only sin and death, and yet one could extend mercy and forgiveness. He realized he was not bound to choose only justice or mercy, as he had done with his daughter. Instead, God called him to be both just and merciful with his daughter.

"Please forgive me, my daughter, for all the years I wasted living in judgement alone."

"Please forgive me, father, for my destructive choices. I drove myself away. I rejected you, our family, the Laws of Moses, and God. But Jesus..."

Her voice broke. She explained to her father what happened after he left, what Jesus said to her, and then added confidently, "Jesus is the Messiah."

She went on and on about forgiveness, freedom from her dark past, and gratitude for another chance and a fresh start with God. She asked her father for a fresh start together.

They humbly agreed that no one is without sin, no one is blameless before God, and no one could have thrown the first stone. Together, they experienced Jesus' love and forgiveness, marveled at the courage of Jesus to challenge the status quo, and thanked God for newfound freedom from ritual religion that only separated people from God and one another.

The next morning, they sought the rabbi together. They began the new day with a new life, reunited, and reconciled to one another and to God. They found Jesus and followed Him. As they listened to His teachings, they became His disciples and eventually joined others in sharing the good news about Jesus, the Messiah. They forgave each other just as Jesus forgave them and even forgave the Pharisees.

Some Pharisees also humbled themselves and they, too, pursued Jesus with open hearts and minds, hoping to know God and understand His word more fully. Although their intentions were evil, God used the incident for good by allowing Jesus to show them how to do justly, love mercy, and walk humbly with their God.

Explore

- *John 8:1–11* | The First Stone.
- *John 7:24* | Judging based on appearance is not recommended.
- *1 Samuel 16:7* | God is unimpressed by your social media image.
- *Micah 6:8* (NKJV) | What does the Lord require of you?
- *Proverbs 16:18* (NIV) | Who coined the phrase, "pride goes before destruction"?
- *Jeremiah 17:13* (NIV) | Whose name is written in the dust? Inquiring minds want to know.
- *Exodus 20:3–17* | God's Ten Commandments
- *Genesis 50:20* | THE TWIST: God means it for good!

Reflect

- How do we judge correctly without being judgmental?
- How did Jesus judge correctly?
- How might devotion to God become a substitute for love of God?
- What does "pride goes before destruction" mean?
- How can something bad turn out to be good?

Imagine

Imagine how you would feel if Jesus invited you to join Him for lunch today. His treat! You might wonder, how can I look my best for Jesus? Is it formal? Business casual? Knowing Jesus, it's "come as you are!"

There is a private room with a glowing fireplace. Jesus is waiting for you and as you arrive, He stands to greet you with a hug and a smile. Suddenly, you feel like you are the guest of honor. Jesus compliments your big wooly overcoat and asks if you would like to take it off because it's quite warm inside. Turns out, your coat is hiding something that you feel embarrassed about.

The coat represents your public reputation and the image that everyone sees. What is hidden under the coat represents your private self that no one else sees.

You have a choice now as you sit with Jesus. Will you take off the oversized coat that conceals your inner self? Will you let Jesus see you as you are? Will you let Jesus see your heart?

Take as much time as you need to unbutton and unzip that protective layer. Set it aside. Let Jesus see you. He loves you and sees the good in you. He is pleased that you trust Him to see your inner self. He approves! He likes you, and in fact, He loves you. Just as you are. Oh, and that thing that you are embarrassed about, He sees that too. He offers forgiveness and a fresh start. He gives you a few pointers on how to avoid that thing in the future. Thank Jesus that you don't have to hide or pretend with Him. He sees you and He loves you.

Nothing in all creation is hidden from God's sight.
Everything is uncovered and laid bare before the eyes of him
to whom we must give account.

Hebrews 4:13 (NIV)

Deborah's Victory

Do not merely listen to the word,
and so deceive yourselves.
Do what it says.

James 1:22 NIV

A Publication of Papyrus Press (Circa 1150 BCE)

D eborah is a respected Judge and Prophetess. A national and spiritual leader for our time, she lives in the Hill Country of Ephraim, north of Jerusalem. I am embedded with her as she prepares an offensive campaign to free our nation from the despot Canaanite king, Jabin. As a journalist and historian, and now as a war correspondent, I submit the facts and details of the events that transpired as I witnessed them.

Our forefathers entered the Promised Land about 250 years ago. During that time, Israel has seen both its leaders and people cycle from holiness to disobedience and back to holiness again. Deborah aspires to lead the tribes of Israel in obeying and trusting God as King.

I meet Deborah as she sits calmly on a colorful woven rug under a date palm, known locally as "The Palm Tree of

Deborah." She regularly listens and teaches in this open-air venue where people can hear and be heard, and she is known for issuing fair and just solutions in response to the concerns people bring.

As a prophetess and judge, she speaks on behalf of God, and people accept her instructions and decisions as the will of God. The location is hot during the day, and the shade sparse, but that doesn't stop the steady stream of people bringing personal and corporate grievances.

I listen as many express concern about the brutal king and his army commander, Sisera. For twenty years, Sisera and the iron-fisted king have employed their 900 iron chariots in making our roads and countryside unsafe.

Deborah has called a man named Barak—from Kedesh in the far northern province of Naphtali—to a meeting under her palm tree. Since Kedesh is located near the Canaanite's stronghold camp, this selection of Barak seems an interesting choice. Perhaps Barak has information about our enemy. He arrives and joins us under her palm tree.

"The Lord, the God of Israel, commands you," Deborah tells him, "Go! Take 10,000 men of Naphtali and Zebulun and lead the way to Mount Tabor. I will lure Sisera with his chariots and troops to the Kishon River and give them into your hands."

Barak balks.

"If you go with me, I will go," he counters, "but if you don't go with me, I won't go."

Deborah pauses. She speaks for God. She has faithfully conveyed His message directing a specific person to a specific task with a sincere promise of victory. Barak's response is as much a challenge to God as to her.

I'm not sure what Barak was thinking. Some of my sources think maybe he was uncomfortable with the strategy coming from a woman and that he feared the plan would fail. Other sources suggested he doubted his own ability to fulfill the plan. Still others wondered if it was his immense respect for Deborah that compelled him to seek her accompaniment in the battle. As a Prophet, she carried the presence and blessing of God with her. He may have believed he needed her with him to secure the victory.

"Very well, I will go with you," Deborah says. "But because of the course you are taking, the honor will not be yours, for the Lord will deliver Sisera into the hands of a woman."

I accompany Deborah and Barak as they trek north to Kedesh, gather 10,000 men, and ascend Mount Tabor.

When Sisera learns that Barak has gathered an army, he gathers his own forces, along with all 900 chariots, to challenge Barak's. As Sisera's army approaches, Deborah suddenly cries out to Barak, "Go! This is the day the LORD has given Sisera into your hands. The LORD has gone ahead of you!" I watch from above as Barak and his 10,000 men rush down the mountain.

The Kishon River below flows perennially throughout the year. However, seasonally dry sections are intermingled with clinging mud, bottomless mire, and tangled grass. During the rainy season, the mountainous landscape channels water into raging torrents that leave behind rich layers of soil which offer abundant nutrition for crops but serve as poor roadways.

As I watch, it seems that God had indeed gone before Israel by sending rain that has swollen the river and prepared mud traps for Sisera's heavy iron chariots. Barak and his men shout praise to God as they secure the promised victory.

But Sisera has disappeared. We receive reports from the battlefield that they found his abandoned iron chariot along the muddy riverbank. Another report arrives that Sisera was seen fleeing on foot away from the battle.

On a hunch, I head toward the great tree of Zaanannim near Kedesh where Heber the Kenite, a relative of Moses, has settled his clan. Although Heber lives in the province of Naphtali, he is no friend of Deborah and Barak, nor of Barak's people, and so, he chooses to live apart from the others in his province. He has a peace treaty with Jabin, the tyrant king, to secure protection for his family. It seemed plausible to me that Sisera might seek interim safety with a friendly partner.

According to my sources, Heber lives in self-isolation from the other Kenites of his tribe because he has issues with people descended from the father-in-law of Moses. Heber's feud stretches back to before our people entered the Promised Land and might have something to do with Moses's sister Miriam's issues with Moses' wife. I'm not sure if the dispute included Moses' father-in-law, too, but there are obvious seeds of dissention that have taken root in the Promised Land.

I arrive just in time to stake out a position nearby before I see Sisera stumbling frantically toward the encampment. Heber's wife, Jael, sees him and goes out to meet him.

"Come right in," she says. "Don't be afraid."

Exhausted, he welcomes her invitation.

"I'm thirsty. Please give me some water."

I watch as she steps out to retrieve a skin of milk instead and hear him gulping the refreshing liquid.

"Stand in the doorway of the tent," he instructs. "If someone comes by and asks if anyone is here, tell them 'No.'"

Before long, I hear snoring.

I suspect Jael has tucked Sisera in, under a comforting woolen blanket, and he has fallen asleep certain he has escaped the consequences of his humiliating defeat safe inside the tent of an ally. Like most of the tribes, the Kenites practice hospitality and protection of passers-by, graciously offering shelter and nourishment when needed.

I've seen a lot of gruesome things as a war correspondent. What happened next, I only partly see, but memorably hear.

I watch as Jael calmly exits the tent, selects a long wooden tent peg from a stack outside, grabs a hammer from the tool bench, and reenters. Shortly thereafter, I hear pounding. The first strikes sound more like crunching, then transition to the more familiar sound of pounding a peg into the ground.

Jael reemerges to stand sentry in the doorway. I notice the snoring has stopped. An eerie, but peaceful, silence ensues.

I hear approaching noises as Jael watches in the distance. Barak soon arrives obviously pursuing the trail of his enemy, Sisera. Jael exits and greets Barak.

"Come. I will show you the man you're looking for."

She leads him into the tent and recounts what happened.

"So, let me get this straight," Barak summarizes. "You put him to sleep with warm milk and a blanket and then drove a tent peg through his temple and killed him."

I recall Deborah's prophetic words, "The honor will not be yours, for the LORD will deliver Sisera into the hands of a woman." When she first said it, I thought she meant herself. But here is Jael, standing with Barak, and it is she who has calmly defeated Sisera, a brutal enemy of Israel. Before long, I watch and listen as Deborah and Barak honor Jael singing in victory celebration, "Most blessed of women be Jael, the wife of Heber the Kenite, most blessed of tent-dwelling women."

Deborah soon returns to sit on her woolen rug in the sparse shade under her palm tree—a symbol of justice. She continues to offer just decisions and instructions to people who seek her guidance. She teaches people to walk with God and obey his ways and she helps them with the difficulties they sometimes face in living with one another. Under her leadership, we have secured justice for our people through the victory over the oppressive king Jabin and his commander, Sisera. With God as King, we are enjoying peace in the land.

Explore

- *Judges 4 and 5* | THE SAGA: Victory for Deborah, Barak, and a woman named Jael.
- *Judges 2:18* | The LORD is with Judge Deborah.
- *Judges 1:16* (NIV) | Moses' father-in-law is a Kenite.
- *Judges 4:11* (NASB) | Heber, is a Kenite descendant, an ally with Deborah's enemy.

Reflect

- What might be some of the reasons Jael betrayed Sisera in her tent?
- What is justice? Do you see justice in this story? Do you see injustice?
- How might seeds of dissention cause someone to live in isolation?
- Can we know if we have seeds of dissention in our lives?
- What can we do to uproot weeds of dissention?

Imagine

Do you long for justice today? Is it personal justice that you seek? Do you want justice for your family, or justice in your community? Injustice is a painful burden to carry alone.

Picture the Court of God. This is your time to bring forth your complaint. State your case. Produce your evidence. Draw your conclusions. The Judge is listening.

Would you like a verdict today? Be assured, the Judge has heard you and will issue a judgment—maybe not today, but in due time. Will you wait? If there is a continuance, then there will be a delay in the decision. Will you wait on the Judge?

Gather up all your documents and reports. Stack up your legal filings and exhibits. Collect your testimonies and records of the injustice against you and your community. Bring it all forth to the Judge's bench. It's nearly impossible to simply leave it in the hands of the Judge because it feels so passive. But you somehow manage to release the stacks of evidence. It's in His hands now.

This Judge is guaranteed to be fair and impartial. He is the final Judge. The ultimate Judge. He is God. You have brought your complaint and appealed to the highest court. It's time to rest your case.

For the LORD is our judge, the LORD is our lawgiver,
the LORD is our king; He will save us.

Isaiah 33:22 (NASB)

Chapter 8

We Called a Meeting

The Trial of Mary and Martha

*Let us therefore make every effort to do
what leads to peace and to mutual edification.*

Romans 14:19 (NIV)

W hispers and sideways glances; hushed voices; a sheepish smile. Gossip. It's as old as dirt, and possibly older. It leaves a mark that can be resistant to stain remover. No one wants to be the topic of a juicy morsel of gossip, but then again, we don't usually get the choice.

Mary and Martha were well known sisters in the town of Bethany. Everyone knew they were like two peas in a pod. Mary excelled in creating a warm and inviting environment, and as a gracious hostess she tended to the personal and relational needs of her guests. Martha excelled in logistics and in the kitchen, and she focused her attention on the physical needs of her friends and family. Together, they were a great team. Mary and Martha worked together seamlessly to provide warm hospitality for all who entered their home. You couldn't imagine one without the other, just like good and bad, hot and cold, or right and wrong.

How did the women of Bethany become so divided about this dynamic duo? Some sat comfortably on Team Mary while the rest squirmed on Team Martha. Accusations arose from both sides. Their brother Lazarus, along with all the men, grew weary of the back-and-forth debate. A group of us finally organized a committee of influential women to get to the bottom of it and settle once and for all what happened that day in Bethany to cause such a ruckus. We invited Mary and Martha to testify, or rather speak, to our committee on their own behalf.

According to my notes of the proceedings, things seem to have fallen apart soon after Jesus and his followers arrived unexpectedly at the home the two sisters shared with their brother. Martha explained that she was the one who greeted Jesus with a grateful hug and a holy kiss and she invited Jesus and his followers to join them for dinner in their home. As the group arrived, Martha noticed the number of men and women following Jesus had increased since the last time they visited. Instinctively, she counted heads as they entered the house.

Mary countered that she and Lazarus were in the courtyard when Jesus arrived. She was the one, she insisted, not Mary, who invited Jesus and his followers to dinner.

They agreed that they met in the kitchen to make plans. Martha confirmed that she basically decided to cook everything in the house while Mary sent word to nearby friends to bring more food. Meanwhile, while Martha scurried around cleaning, cooking, and gathering items needed for dinner, Mary attended to arranging the seating pillows and cushions and greeting guests. She admitted that she soon found herself immersed in happy reunions, conversations with friends, and listening to Jesus.

Martha confessed that the numerous tasks required to prepare dinner for everyone weighed heavily upon her. Her feet and back ached, her nerves were frazzled, and the kitchen soon filled with platters of food. But Mary disappeared.

"When I peeked out from the kitchen and saw Mary just sitting there at Jesus' feet listening intently to every word he said, I lost it."

She admitted impulsively darting straight to Jesus and exclaiming, "Lord, don't you care that my sister has left me to do the work by myself? Tell her to help me!"

Jesus responded, "Martha, Martha, you are worried and upset about many things, but few things are needed—or indeed only one. Mary has chosen what is better, and it will not be taken away from her."

His words stung, and she felt embarrassed. She admitted that one of her first thoughts was, *Fine then! I can just sit here, too, and everyone can go fix their own food, or go hungry!*"

"However," she continued quietly, "I knew what Jesus meant as soon as he spoke the words. He saw my heart and understood my request as a veiled accusation."

It was as if she told Jesus, "You don't care about me," which she knew in her heart was not true. Furthermore, it sounded like she was telling her dear Lord Jesus what to do when she demanded he tell Mary to help her in the kitchen.

"I dishonored Jesus in my desperation. Like Mary, I needed to stop fretting and spend time with Jesus." She hung her head with a look of regret, embarrassment, and shame.

Mary spoke up in her defense.

"I could, and should, have helped Martha more. I knew there was a lot to do and that everyone was hungry. But, once

I was engaged, I just couldn't pull myself away. Honestly, I just forgot at that point. I love Jesus and respect and admire his wise teaching. We've never heard anything like it!"

At that point, we all noticed that they were holding and patting each other's hands. They understood each other, needed each other, and loved each other. I think most of us understood, too. We saw our misjudgment of these two loving sisters and how unnecessarily divided they had become and how unfairly divided we became supposedly on their behalf.

We also saw ourselves in both sisters. We have all fussed over too many concerns, and other times ignored the needs of people closest to us. Worst of all, we knew that at times we thought maybe we could make the Lord step in and do what we wanted, usually to make things easier for us.

Team Mary and Team Martha joined together that day as One Team with a new purpose. We noted the admonition from the Proverbs, "Get wisdom, get understanding. The beginning of wisdom is this: Get wisdom. Though it cost all you have, get understanding."

We determined that would surely save us a lot of time and trouble in the future. We agreed to help each other learn and apply the wise teachings of Jesus to our everyday lives, and to show understanding to one another. We also decided to try and listen to each other's advice if we started to go off track. And just like that, Jesus brought us together!

Explore

- *Luke 10:38–42* | Hospitality is exhausting and exhilarating.
- *Proverbs 4:5–7* (NIV) | TO DO LIST: 1) Get Wisdom, and 2) Get Understanding.
- *1 Thessalonians 5:26* (NIV) | A kiss on the cheek is a friendly greeting.

Reflect

- Do you identify with Mary? Martha? Both? Neither?
- Do you think Mary admired Martha in some way?
- Do you think Martha valued something in Mary?
- How do we get wisdom and understanding?

Imagine

Picture yourself strolling down a country road enjoying the company of Jesus. It's a perfectly gorgeous day. Approaching an unexpected fork in the road, you must make a choice. Left, or right? Time passes. It's getting late. Unfortunately, you can't see very far down either one of the paths in the fading sunlight. How do you feel? Have you faced a choice recently, or have you reached a fork in the road in your life today?

How about asking Jesus for His help. Earlier in the day He was telling you, "Ask and it will be given to you" (Matthew 7:7a NIV). Go ahead and ask Him now. "Lord, which way do I go?" Take a breath and wait for His answer.

Jesus would suggest that you to apply wisdom to your choice. With a smile, He explains, "The wisdom that comes from heaven is first of all pure; then peace-loving, considerate, submissive, full of mercy and good fruit, impartial and sincere" (James 3:17 NIV).

Now wonder, which of your options will satisfy the qualification of purity, or peace? Is one choice more, or less, conducive to impartiality? Do either of your options allow for sincerity? Perhaps one path is full of mercy. You might not need to meet all the qualifications at the same time but look for at least one or two ways that your choice will express God's wisdom.

Heavenly Wisdom is a very good litmus test. This is how you can use wisdom to evaluate your options. Wisdom will help you to make the choice, and wisdom will give you understanding as you choose. Jesus has equipped you to make your decision. Take your time to apply wisdom to the paths before you. Will you make a choice now? Left, or right? Jesus would love to continue with you on the road that you choose.

Who is wise and understanding among you?
Let them show it by their good life,
by deeds done in humility
that comes from wisdom.

James 3:13 (NIV)

Chapter 9
Lost and Found

The Prodigal's Mother

*For the Son of Man has come to seek
and to save that which was lost.*

Luke 19:10 (NASB)

I t had been a dreadfully long day. When a family bids a final farewell to a loved one, time stretches interminably. As weariness sets in, loved ones simultaneously long to reach the day's conclusion, all the while resisting that final moment when the sun slips over the horizon and darkness falls. When the slow-motion finally ceases, peace can find room to grow and refresh hearts, minds, bodies, and souls with sweet rest and moments of resolution.

Adira collapsed onto one of the wool pillows scattered about the floor of her tent. She survived the day she dreaded, the earthly separation from her husband of fifty-four years. She married Absalom at age sixteen, and together they grew in love and wisdom as they made a life for themselves and their family. Absalom truly lived up to the meaning of his name: Father of Peace. Through all of life's challenges, peace defined Absalom's influence on his family and community. He left behind a legacy of peace by the way he lived his life. Now, in his absence, Adira searched to discover if his peace was still available for her in her sorrow.

As she rested and drew strength from happy memories of her life with Absalom, she smiled ever so slightly. The spark of a twinkle shone from her dark eyes. One after another, we women who gathered to comfort her began to speak softly, struggling to find just the right words. Adira was an honored and respected woman in our community and we were curious as to how she could smile on one of the worst days of her life. We knew her and remembered that she had faced difficult and painful days before, and yet, she still seemed able to find a moment of joy amid sadness.

"Absalom was a good man," one ventured.

"A good father, wise and strong in faith," another offered.

"Will you tell us a story about Absalom?" another queried.

Adira did not reply or even move. The silence grew longer and more uncomfortable. Had we pressed too hard?

No. She was searching, scanning decades of memories for a special one to share, to remind everyone just how Absalom lived his life and how the lovingkindness of God can be found in the darkest of times. Her smile broadened, and she adjusted herself to sit up a bit more to share a most treasured memory.

"As you know, we are shepherds and have been for many generations. We love our sheep and would give our lives to protect our flocks. All of you enjoy the fine wool from our sheep, the finest in the hill country, I believe."

The group nodded in agreement. Most were adorned with shawls made of the softest and most pure wool one could find in Judea. Absalom and Adira's flocks were well-managed, and the high quality of their wool widely known and respected.

"One spring, Absalom took the sheep to a new, freshly sprouted field in the east. After a dry winter, the sheep longed for tender green spring grass. I remember we had exactly 100 sheep in our flock that year."

"Was that the time Absalom lost one?"

Adira recognized the speaker but ignored her tactless assertion and thinly veiled accusation. Adira's name meant "strong, mighty, or majestic," and she chose to act in strength and extend grace to the one who posed the awkward question.

"Yes, we lost one that year. Absalom took them out to graze and our two sons planned to join him to help guide the sheep to the unfamiliar pasture. Morning chores delayed Benjamin, our oldest. By the time David returned from the market and they met up to travel to the eastern pasture together, they discovered the flock unattended. Their father was nowhere to be found. They counted the sheep several times and kept arriving at the same number: ninety-nine. You can imagine how their hearts sank when they realized that wherever their father was, their delayed arrival put the flock in danger and may have also endangered the missing sheep and their father. Finally, many long hours later, the boys recognized the shape of their father heading in their direction. As he drew closer, they realized he had something draped across his broad shoulders."

She paused. "Any guesses?"

"The lost sheep?" I ventured.

"Yes! When he realized a lamb was missing and alone, Absalom went to search for it. The boys enjoyed a happy reunion with their father, as did the lamb with the flock. That night, we celebrated our good fortune with family and friends, as some of you may remember."

Several nodded. Celebrating joyous events with others created special memories, and some remembered that one.

"However," Adira continued as she furrowed her brow, dropped her voice, and relinquished her smile, "the next day, David announced his intention to leave home and our blessed life of farming and shepherding behind. Not only that, but he also wanted his share of the family inheritance to start a new life in the city.

"Absalom and I were heartbroken. Why would our son betray his family and our customs to leave and begin a new life somewhere else without us? Hadn't we loved him enough? We named him David, which means 'Beloved,' and we always treasured him as a blessing to our family. We wondered if he was jealous of his first-born older brother. While we had difficulty making sense of this terrible news, once we realized David's determination to move forward, only one final act of love remained. Absalom assessed our entire estate, evaluated David's prospective inheritance, converted enough assets to money, and gave David his portion. He very quickly gathered his things and left to apparently get as far away from us as he could. We lost our youngest son that day."

Tears welled up over eyelids, rolled down cheeks, and leapt unashamedly onto whatever lay below. Adira's transparent, raw words touched all of us, not just her. She remembered the confusion and pain as she watched David leave, never once looking back. We shared her pain in motionless silence; it seemed no one could breathe.

Words cannot sufficiently express some hard and painful thoughts. Some events are too complex to comprehend. Adira reflected on her prayerful attempts to comprehend the abrupt departure of her beloved David. After many sleepless nights and weary days, she finally surmised what it may have felt like for David, the forever little brother standing in the tall shadow of Benjamin. He loved his big brother, as brothers do. But he also envied his brother for the position he held in the family by what some simply call an accident of birth; he was first. Benjamin would always be first. It was his destiny.

Furthermore, as if nothing could be more daunting than living in the shadow of a model big brother, Absalom cast a sizeable shadow as an ideal father with impossibly high standards. David loved and respected him despite feeling that no one could ever measure up to his legendary reputation.

While it is an honor to be respected, esteemed for your wisdom and success, there can also be a price to pay for such an elevated reputation. The fault is not with the one so revered, but a natural effect in a fallen world on the people who live within the circle of an appearance of near perfection.

Of course no one can choose how others respond to them. Benjamin never intended to harm the self-esteem of his little brother. Absalom certainly never meant to wound his son by his own lifestyle choices. Not at all! He rather hoped to serve as a positive role model for both sons. Unfortunately, David fell victim to covetousness, jealousy, and adverse comparison to his brother and father. The sum of his faults and flaws added up to a deficit, with interest compounded daily, resulting in a debt of confidence not easily overcome. He saw only one way out—withdraw and close the account. He intended to leave for good and abandon the rest behind.

Adira took a long, deep breath, and continued her story.

"David disappeared from our lives. We didn't know where he went, but I prayed for him as often as he came to mind, basically all day every day. I hoped he was well but eventually heard that one of my greatest fears had come to pass. Between wanton spending, wild living, and shady dealings, he lost his inheritance, along with his dignity. Broke and beset and amid a severe famine, he was finally able to secure a job—degrading, unclean work—feeding filthy pigs of a man of unclean heart and hands. My beloved son became financially, physically, and spiritually bankrupt."

Adira's words added a new layer of horror on top of the pain and sorrow, along with the joys, recounted thus far.

"After David left, Benjamin labored hard doing double duty due to his brother's absence. He accepted his position and role with great seriousness and resolve. 'Son of the Right Hand' seemed like a fitting name for a first-born son, and now every day we could see how he embraced his responsibilities with diligence as he lived up to his name and added to his father's reputation every day.

"One spring day about a year after David left, I wanted to express my gratitude to Benjamin and let him know that I noticed how hard he was working and without complaint. In my heart, I wanted to bless his day with a little gift from my treasure box. Even though money was tight since we sent David away with his portion, I had managed to stash away ten silver coins—each worth about a day's wages—to build up funds toward some future expense."

We already respected Adira's gentleness, hard work, and wisdom. The private revelation that she disciplined herself to regularly save money even when resources were tight only added to our admiration.

"Yet, when I opened my box, I only counted nine coins."

Eyebrows raised. *What happened to the other coin? David couldn't have stolen it, since he was already gone. Did someone else take it? Or maybe she just misplaced it?*

"What did you do?" we demanded. We knew that, though sons may, coins don't run away by themselves.

"I cleaned my tent. Very carefully, and very thoroughly."

We nodded. *Adira was so practical—that totally made sense. Why jump to other conclusions without evidence?*

"The best thing to do when you lose something valuable at home is to light a lamp and carefully clean. Best case scenario is you will find what is lost. Worse case, you end up with a freshly cleaned home!"

Okay, add funny to Adira's list of admirable qualities.

"Did you find it?"

"Yes, yes I did." She smiled again.

"I was so excited! I skipped out of the tent like a happy baby goat, and calling out to anyone and everyone, 'I found it! I found it! It was lost, but I searched for it, and I found it!' I was so overjoyed, and relieved. I was thankful to God, who sees me and cares for me, who protects and provides for us all. I felt like God cared enough for me to bless me so I could in turn bless Benjamin."

She paused. Her face transitioned from one of happiness to one of extreme delight. Her eyes nearly glowed as she leaned her head back and laughed, her broadly smiling lips exposing nearly all her teeth in a moment of pure pleasure.

"Unknown to me, my moment of joy was about to increase exponentially. While rejoicing, I heard Absalom shouting and celebrating, too. I thought he was happy because he heard about me finding my lost coin. But he wasn't looking at me. He was looking away. In fact, he was running away, shouting

85

and waving his arms in the air. *What in the world?* I wondered *What could possibly be happening now?* And then I saw him. Absalom was running toward a strangely familiar person off in the distance. I gasped. I knew this person's gait, his manner. I had not seen it for a while, and it lacked its former vibrance, but I knew my own son, even from a distance. David. Was he coming home? It looks like David is coming home!

"I watched as my compassionate and forgiving husband ran to greet our son. I don't know if I ever saw him run as fast as he did that day. As I ran toward them, David's poor condition and weak stagger became very apparent. By the time I reached them, Absalom was weeping, I was weeping, and David was sobbing like a baby. Finally, as his tears, heaves, and sobs began to subside, David knelt.

"'Father, what a fool I am. I lost all my inheritance, my identity, and you and my family. I have wronged you. I have disrespected our traditions and our God and am unworthy to be welcomed back into this family. But, if you have any compassion for me left in your heart, please allow me to serve in your household as a hired worker. I know I've disqualified myself from being the son of a man of peace. I am willing to make amends every day for the pain I have caused you, our family, and our God.'"

Adira interjected commentary into her own narrative.

"Now, as you all know, Absalom was a man of patience, peace, and strong faith. He wisely allowed David to say what he had in his mind and weighing on his heart at the time. He stood there while David opened the floodgates holding back his pain and suffering. He listened as David recounted how he lost himself in our home and found himself in the wilderness. David admitted the buildup of envy and resentment led him to bitterness and his decision to depart. He acknowledged that only after he lost everything did he understand what he lost. In that moment, David's wisdom mirrored his father's."

Several women interrupted.

"What did Absalom say?"

"Did he scold him?"

"Absolutely not! Absalom cried the whole time David was talking and giving his heartfelt speech. I think Absalom was only thinking that his lost son finally came to his senses and decided to return home. He was rejoicing in our son's restoration to our family, community, and God. Joy replaced sorrow, repentance overcame foolishness, and forgiveness opened the door to beginning to heal deep wounds."

"Was that the day your family hosted a big feast at your place?" one of the younger women wondered aloud. "I was just a child, but that was one of the best celebrations I ever remember going to in our community."

"Yes, yes!" Adira replied. "Absalom jumped into party mode very quickly. He set workers in motion bringing our best robe out for David to wear, putting our family ring on his finger, giving him new sandals for his feet, and killing the fattened calf specially reserved for feasting."

"I remember," another recalled, "Absalom ran around the village announcing, 'Come celebrate with me. My son was lost and now is found. We thought him dead, but look, he lives!'"

"What about Benjamin?" another queried.

"Ah, yes, Benjamin."

Adira clasped her hands, accented with a slight wringing, pursing frown, raised eyebrows, and head shake.

"By the time Benjamin arrived from working out in the fields, tending crops and trees, and caring for the animals, we were already celebrating. While he was dirty, tired, and ready to eat well-deserved food and enjoy hard-earned rest, we were already dancing, singing, and preparing for a grand feast.

"When he inquired as to what was happening, one our staff informed him about what we all thought was great news, 'Your brother David has returned! Your father is putting on a huge celebration and has ordered us to kill and prepare the fattened calf for the feast!'"

Several nodded sideways in anticipation. *Sibling rivalry can show its face at the most inopportune time.* Our faces reflected her darkening demeanor as she continued.

"My dear friends and sisters," Adira confessed, "only one thing could dampen my joy that day. Benjamin surprised me, and disappointed me. Rather than share our delight, he responded with anger. Even as hungry as I'm sure he was, he refused to join the celebration and precious reunion with his only brother. Bitterness and resentment that had taken root in his heart exploded out in harsh words and angry actions. The very idea of compassion and forgiveness seemed to enrage him. Absalom tried to understand his son's resentment and cold heart. Finally, Benjamin poured out his feelings.

"Without holding anything back, he complained loudly and forcefully for the first time that he felt it horribly unfair that he had to slave over the family chores and business the whole time his younger brother was off delighting himself in feasting and luxury. He felt that we never appreciated his unquestioning loyalty, especially when compared to David's weaselly actions. He wanted to know how we could celebrate his disloyalty when it was him, Benjamin, who was the loyal son most deserving of celebration and public recognition. He demanded to know, 'When and where is MY feast? Where is

MY robe and MY ring and MY fattened calf?' The fury and bitterness that exploded from the deep recesses of his clouded mind and chilled heart made quite an impression."

Adira sighed long and audibly. We all stared at her in hushed silence as she continued.

"Absalom was the wisest, kindest man I ever knew. I marvel at my great fortune to have lived such a beautiful life with him for 54 years. After Benjamin's tirade that day, it seemed as if the earth stood still. Finally, Absalom responded.

"'Benjamin, I love you. I have always loved you and always will. You have been a deeply loyal, good, and faithful son serving the family and fulfilling your rightful responsibilities. David already received his inheritance, so everything I own is yours. Everything you are taking care of so well is all yours! You are my son, my first-born, my right hand. I depend on you and am immensely thankful for you. If I have neglected to tell you this, I regret my error and ask you to forgive me. Your place in my heart is secure and irreplaceable.'

"I watched Benjamin as Absalom talked. I saw his face slowly began to soften and his hands began to release from clinching so tightly. His father's words of love, affirmation, regret, and repentance reached their mark. I rejoiced as they smiled at one another for the first time in a long time and finally embraced in swirling emotions of love, forgiveness, and restoration. Although Absalom attempted to then try and explain more fully why he felt so compelled to celebrate David's restoration, Benjamin interrupted him."

"Father. I understand. David was lost, like that sheep you rescued the day before he announced he intended to leave us. Now that he is found, it is good and right to celebrate his rescue and restoration. I get it. Sheep get lost and do stupid things. A good shepherd—like you—will do anything to bring them home safely and celebrate with great joy when they do."

Adira's face beamed again.

"That day we celebrated the restoration of both sons. And it was my dear Absalom who showed us how to forgive and extend grace. Peace enveloped our home again as we each found God's peace in our hearts."

Calmness filled Adira's tent. It is no simple task to tell the story of one person. Their lives are often tangled with the lives of others. Stories are messy, and complicated, just like people. Adira seemed grateful for the opportunity to share her story with dear, close friends. I'm sure she felt hopeful that others would see that the lovingkindness of God can still be found in the darkest of times, even if one feels that all is lost.

She offered us the opportunity to reflect on wisdom found in the Psalms, that just as an earthly father like Absalom would have compassion on his son, so our heavenly Father has compassion on us, His children. She even offered a prayer for us that we would know and believe that our heavenly Father sees each of us and is ready to forgive any who turn toward Him and seek restoration in the family of God. She recalled the image of Absalom returning with the lamb over his shoulder and noted that, if necessary, our Father will search for us, find us, and carry us safely home. Then, our Father and all the heavens will celebrate with joy indescribable over each one who returns home to the family of God and to our heavenly Father.

Explore

- *Luke 15* | A trio of stories to make the same point: We are worthy to be found.

    - 1 sheep/100 sheep = 1% found: Good!
    - 1 coin/10 coins = 10% found: Better!!
    - 1 son/2 sons = 50% found: Best!!!

- *Psalm 37:37* | INVESTMENT ADVICE: Living in peace will pay off in the end!

- *Proverbs 20:21* | Beware! A hasty start can lead to an unfortunate finish.

- *Psalm 103:13* | God is a compassionate father to us.

- *Job 28:24* | Nowhere to run, nowhere to hide. God sees it all.

- *Zephaniah 3:17* | God is so delighted about you that He is going to sing.

- *Luke 15:10* | Party in heaven when even one person turns back to God.

Reflect

- What does it mean to be lost?

- The father in our story, Absalom, rejoiced over finding his lost sheep and he rejoiced over finding his lost son. What can we learn about God, our heavenly Father, and how He feels about us if we are lost?

- The mother in our story, Adira, searches for and finds her lost coin. If God were to search for you, how would God find you? How long will he search?

- Both mother and father rejoiced over finding that which was lost: one sheep, one coin, and one son. What is Jesus trying to tell us in these repetitious parables?

Imagine

Lost. We've all been there. Whether it's just a few minutes or if it feels like forever, lost is an uncomfortable feeling. Found. That's a relief.

Can you picture a time when you lost something valuable like your keys? You searched high and low until you (hopefully) found them.

Do you wonder if God cares that much for you? Would He search high and low for you, even if you were hiding from Him? Go ahead and ask Him now, "Would you, Lord, be as devoted as the father who was looking for his sheep? Or would you, God, be as determined as the mother who was looking for her coin? Lord, would you search the horizon for me just as the father did for his son?"

Wait for the Lord to answer.

If you can believe that God "sees everything under the heavens" then that means He sees you. You are never truly lost to God. If you feel lost, rest assured that Jesus will find you. He will never get tired of looking for you. He will look for you until you know that you are found.

Rejoice with me; I have found my lost sheep.

Luke 15:6 (NIV)

Chapter 10
Wait For It

Hannah's Hope

But as for me, I watch in hope for the Lord,
I wait for God my Savior; my God will hear me.

Micah 7:7 NIV

Hannah rose quietly before dawn and stepped softly outside into the grey mist. Once the morning sun filtered into her family tent, moments like this would quickly disappear. As she paused to whisper a prayer to the Lord, she opened her hands to the sky and lifted her face toward heaven and the God who remembers.

For a moment, nothing else seemed to exist beyond this experience in God's presence. She worshipped God for His kind mercy and asked for His continued blessing on her family. As the sun continued to rise, she faced the day with hope, basked in the warmth of the sun on her face that reminded her of the daily faithfulness of her God, and smiled thinking of the blessings that the new day would bring.

Soon enough, life in the tent sprang into action. Chaos ensued as the family awakened and stumbled over one another on the most special day of the year. Hannah and her husband Elkanah, along with their precious sons and daughters, prepared to go to Shiloh to worship the Lord. Peninnah, Elkanah's other wife, and their children would also share the family journey. Each year at this time, Elkanah and his clan honored the Lord with sacrifices and prayers at the tabernacle in Shiloh.

Like busy bees on a spring morning, everyone helped with preparations. From the oldest to the youngest, they all had a job. The adults focused on gathering sacrifices and offerings for the Lord, and all the supplies needed to feed the family while traveling away from home. The children gathered their own possessions, dolls, and blankets to bring the comforts of home on the week-long trip.

While packing, they imagined interesting travelers they might see along the way and wondered what souvenirs they might find as they trekked through the countryside. Though only fourteen miles away, the annual family adventure followed twisting hill country paths from Ramathaim and then a well-worn road north to Shiloh, and included camping together under the stars, rain or shine.

Hannah's children looked forward to their annual visit with their big brother, Samuel. He lived at the tabernacle at Shiloh and served as assistant to Eli, the priest. Hannah pictured seeing her first-born and looked forward to giving him a new lovingly woven linen tunic, an outer cloak, and a sturdy leather belt. She packed these items into her travel pack first, along with a soft wool blanket to help keep him warm on cool days and cold nights since the wind blew regularly at Shiloh year-round.

As their large clan departed and the sun began to rise high in the sky, the excitement began to wear off. Weariness and boredom came quickly as the exciting expectations receded with each new plodding step during the early parts of the trip.

"How much longer?" the children whined. "When are we finally getting to Shiloh? I'm hungry. I need to go to the bathroom."

"Would you like the hear a story?" Hannah asked. She knew stories helped pass the time and her children were old enough now to hear this one.

"Oh yes, Eema, please tell us," her oldest daughter begged. Hannah smiled and began.

"Before you were born, your father and I were young and in love and hoped for a big, beautiful family. However, years passed as we built a life together, but had no children, not even one. During the same time, your father and Peninnah had many children. Naturally, Peninnah was very happy, and proud of herself and her children. But I was very sad. I felt inside as if a thorn pierced my soul, like the hurt when a thorn sticks your finger. But I was about to find out that God can heal the broken-hearted."

Hannah paused to reflect as she gazed into the inquisitive faces of her lovely children. Then she continued.

"Each year, just like this year, we traveled to Shiloh to worship the Lord—me, your father, Peninnah, and her children. Even though I kept a smile on my face and treated Peninnah and her children well, my heart hurt inside because I wanted the honor of bringing children into the world and into our family. I felt like I let your father down and was disappointed in myself, too."

Though her children would not like this part of the story, Hannah did not skip over her hurt. As their mother, she considered truth-telling obligatory. Children should learn that there will be troubles in life, as well as learn to hope that God sees us, hears us, and answers our prayers.

"One year at Shiloh, Eli the priest read from the Torah about Noah and the Great Flood. Though surely a frightening experience for them, 'God remembered Noah and all the wild animals and the livestock that were with him in the ark, and he sent a wind over the earth, and the waters receded.' What a wonderful deliverance! When I heard these words, I silently prayed and asked God to remember me, too, and deliver me from my suffering. However, we returned home, and still I had no children.

"Some years later while worshipping at Shiloh, Eli read from the Torah about our father Abraham. 'When God destroyed the cities of the plain, he remembered Abraham, and he brought Lot out of the catastrophe that overthrew the cities where Lot had lived.' This, too, was another miraculous deliverance by our mighty God. As I noticed that God remembered Abraham, I asked God to remember me too. Yet, again, we returned home and I had no children.

"Despite my sadness, we returned to Shiloh faithfully, year after year, to worship the Lord. Then one day, as Eli read from the Torah, my heart ached as I heard about Rachel, Jacob's wife. She, too, was loved by her husband, and yet remained childless, just like me. I think Eli may have even glanced at me as he read from the Torah that God remembered Rachel; he listened to her and enabled her to conceive. She became pregnant and gave birth to a son and said, 'God has taken away my disgrace.' She named him Joseph, and said, 'May the Lord add to me another son.' This miracle pierced my heart. I wondered, if God could remember Rachel, why couldn't he remember me?

"The next morning after we ate and drank our memorial meal at Shiloh, I fell to my knees and whispered prayers of desperation that flowed from my lips like a waterfall over a cliff. Was it too much to ask God to remember me too? I wondered if he indeed heard my prayers, if he listened to me, and if he cared for me. If he could remember Noah, Abraham, and Rachel, maybe he could also remember me and deliver me from the shame of being childless in a family with a rival wife as fruitful as a grapevine."

Tears welled up in her eyes as she recalled her brokenness and utter despair. Then, a smile began to creep from the edges of her lips. She wanted her children to know the full story.

"I made a vow to the Lord in that moment. You know, a vow is a very serious thing. It cannot be broken, or tragedy will come. I vowed, 'If you will only look on your servant's misery and remember me and not forget your servant but give her a son, then I will give him to the Lord for all the days of his life.'

"Sitting on his chair by the doorpost to the tabernacle, Eli saw me weeping and moving my lips but mistook my actions for drunkenness. He harshly rebuked me, but I confessed the truth to him. I was overcome with grief, deeply distressed, and fervently and silently petitioning the Lord. Fortunately, Eli believed me, and said, 'Go in peace; and may the God of Israel grant your petition that you have asked of him.'

"After that, for the first time in many years, I felt at peace in my heart and mind, and my face even showed it. I sensed that the Lord had heard my plea and, in my heart, a tiny ember of faith began to grow into a flame of hope."

Hannah smiled broadly. As she looked into the expectant, radiant eyes of her children, she said, "I think you all know what happened next!"

"Samuel!" they shouted, as their spirits lightened and their steps quickened. As several skipped and walked more briskly, a feeling of celebration came over Hannah and her children.

"Yes, Samuel," Hannah replied. They all loved Samuel and couldn't wait to see him again. Then she continued.

"God remembered me. He gave us Samuel in answer to my prayers and Eli's priestly blessing. So, I remembered God's graciousness and kept my vow to the Lord. I dedicated Samuel, our firstborn, to God. I loved our beautiful boy, our miracle baby. I treasured him, nurtured him, and trained him in the ways of our God. I memorized his smile, his laugh, and all his funny little faces. I tried to teach him everything he would need to know and show him how to live a life of devotion to the Lord. Each day was filled with incredible joy, and at the same time, an awareness of the coming day when I would release Samuel fully into the service of God. Samuel lived in our home and under my care for just a little while. God entrusted me with Samuel, and then I entrusted him to God.

"The first year Samuel was born, I did not go up to Shiloh to worship. But, after I weaned him, we took Samuel to Eli, along with a sacrifice offering: a three-year-old bull, an ephah of flour, and a jug of wine. I presented Samuel to Eli as the child I prayed for and the son God gave me, and we dedicated Samuel to the Lord and left him in Eli's care.

"Every year since then, during our annual trip to Shiloh, Eli prays this blessing over us, 'May the Lord give you children by this woman to take the place of the one she prayed for and gave to the Lord.'

"And now look! There are five of you, my sweet children! You have all filled my heart with love and joy, and each of you is a special gift from the Lord who hears our prayers and remembers us."

As intended, her story helped ease their journey and pass the time. As they rounded the final curve in the road and began to make their way up the winding approach toward the gate at Shiloh, her children ran ahead. They always looked forward to seeing Samuel, and this year they had a deeper appreciation for their mother's sacrifice.

Suddenly, there he was. Samuel must have been watching since he sprinted out from the gate with arms spread wide to greet his family. As he hugged and delightfully swung each of his siblings around in turn, with fresh eyes, they saw their brother more clearly as an answer to prayer, a miracle, and proof that the Lord sees, hears, and remembers. In his presence, they felt the Presence of the Lord, which nurtured their young faith that God would hear their prayers, too. God was with them, just as Samuel was with them, no matter what.

Hannah continued telling her story each year on the way to Shiloh. She delighted as she watched Samuel continue to grow in stature and in favor with the Lord and with people. He was living proof to Hannah that God heard her prayers and remembered her, and her story reinforced this to her family.

Unbeknownst to Hannah, Samuel foreshadowed the divine Child of Promise born around a millennium later in Bethlehem and named "Jesus." Hannah herself foreshadowed his mother, Mary, in the sense that she also watched as her son grew in wisdom and stature and in favor with God and man. Just as Samuel was living proof to Hannah, Jesus was living proof to the entire world that God is willing and able to see our needs, hear our prayers, and remember us for all eternity.

Explore

- *Proverbs 31:25* | Hannah can smile at the future.
- *1 Samuel 1–2* | An intimate view into both the pain of infertility and the joy of childbirth.
- *Psalm 147:3* | Who can we mend a broken heart?
- *Genesis 8:1* | God remembers Noah.
- *Genesis 19:29* | God remembers Abraham.
- *Genesis 30:22–24* | God remembers Rachel, and so he enables her to conceive a child.
- *1 Samuel 1:11* | THE VOW: If you remember me...
- *1 Samuel 2:26* | Samuel grows in favor with the Lord.
- *Luke 2:52* | Jesus grows in favor with God.

Reflect

- What does it mean for a mother to dedicate her child to the Lord? Why would she do this?
- How do we dedicate ourselves to the Lord? What does dedication to the Lord look like?
- How does suffering draw us closer to God?
- What happens when we pull away from God in hard times?
- Where is God when you suffer? How would Hannah answer this question?
- How does God heal the thorns in our hearts?

Imagine

Do you remember hearing that everyone has a Permanent Record? I do. I always wondered; where does that document exist? Now I know. All the days that were ordained for me were written in God's book, even before one of them ever happened (Psalm 139:16b NIV). That's where the record is—in heaven. Come with me on a trip to the Heavenly Hall of Records, and let's go find your section in God's book.

As we arrive at the Entrance, you submit your request, and you alone receive permission to enter your wing of the Heavenly Hall. This is where you must go forward on your own. It is all between you and God now. I wait outside.

Your wing is filled with thousands of file drawers filled with untold pages. God must have recorded everything! Indeed, there is even a section devoted to "Tears" with this inscription, "God has put my tears in His bottle, and in His book" (Psalm 56:8 NASB).

You notice a huge section devoted to "Prayers" and divided into two categories: "Answered" and "Unanswered." Without hesitation you pull open the drawer of "Unanswered Prayers." It is completely empty! Yanking open the drawer of "Answered Prayers" you find it jam packed and overflowing!

You turn to God and ask, "Why is the drawer for the 'Unanswered Prayers' empty?"

You seem to remember plenty of times He did not answer your prayers, and you describe to God how you felt about it.

What does He say to you?

Maybe He says something like this: "It may be hard to hear, My child, but sometimes the answer is an easy 'Yes' and sometimes it's an easy 'No.' Please be assured that when I say 'No' it's because I have something much better for you, or I want to protect you from unintended consequences. But there is always an answer. My answer flows from my deep love for you and My eternal perspective of what is best for you. Perhaps the hardest answer to accept is 'Wait.' Sometimes I want you to wait for the right time, and the right way for Me to bless you beyond your wildest dreams. Sometimes you underestimate what I would do for you and ask for too little. And sadly, sometimes you misunderstand and feel like 'Wait' means 'No' when I really mean 'No, not yet.' Believe Me, I will always answer you because I love you. Nothing can separate you from My love" (Romans 8:38–39)."

As you exit and we leave the Heavenly Hall of Records together, I pray that you have gained some clarity and better understand prayer. Like Hannah, I hope you feel sure that God remembers you and answers your prayers. I think you do, especially since when I ask you about unanswered prayers you tease me, "Sometimes you just have to wait for it."

Lord, I wait for you;
you will answer, Lord my God.

Psalm 38:15 (NIV)

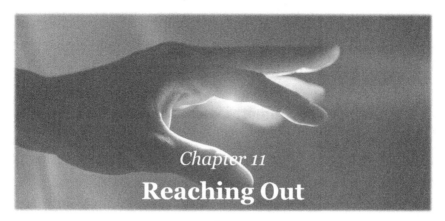

Chapter 11
Reaching Out

I Touched Him

*Things that are impossible with people
are possible with God.*

Luke 18:27 (NASB)

I have been shooed away countless times in my life. I have experienced so much disdain, scorn, and exclusion. If God started with a dark canvas and only added one shining star to the sky every time someone spurned me, the night would appear as bright as day.

I once had a family, felt love, and experienced belonging in my community. But, for twelve long years, I lived with rejection, loneliness, and despair, and those years took a toll on my body, my mind, and eventually on my spirit. I used to fear every daybreak, dread every sunlit hour, and shrink into anxious distress every night. But, one day, everything changed.

It began like any other day for me: lonely, afraid, and shunned. But, while navigating the shadowy fringes of my community, I overheard the news about a remarkable man traveling throughout our region. Some called him a prophet, others a man of God, and others a miracle worker. I was surprised to hear these stories because no one important bothers to visit us here; we are poor and rarely host special people or events.

According to one rumor, something incredible happened when he and his friends crossed the Sea of Galilee in a fishing boat on their way to the region of the Gerasenes. As happens on occasion due to the wind traveling across the high ridge on one side, dropping down to cross the lake, and then going back up across the ridge on the other side, a sudden tempest arose. The strong winds and violent waves threatened to capsize their boat. Though he was asleep at the time up under the small deck, his friends were so afraid for their lives that they desperately woke him up. When he awoke, he got up and, as the story goes, he commanded the wind and the waves to be still, and the storm immediately subsided. It was told that he posed a question to his friends, "Where is your faith?" They were so filled with both amazement and fear, that as soon as they landed safely ashore, they told this story to anyone who would listen and it spread far and wide. It all seemed quite farfetched to me. *How could something like that happen? It's never happened before!*

I heard another rumor about the demon-possessed man who lived in the region of the Gerasenes on the other side of the lake. I know him, or at least, I knew him once upon a time before demons took control of his life and destroyed everything he had. His name is Ari and he was my childhood friend. Like me, he too lived alone. He dwelled in solitary places in the wilderness, finding shelter in cold dark tombs, naked, and apart from the people who love him. Like me, he was lonely, suffering, and in need of deliverance.

This prophet, named Jesus, spoke to the cruel demons who tormented my friend. Jesus commanded them to come out of him. Despite their desperate objections, the demons were forced to leave my friend. The legion of demons entered a nearby herd of pigs, which our laws declare unclean, and then the entire herd ran off the hillside and drowned in the Sea. When the people in town heard about it, they were furious that they may have lost their livelihood and investment in the herd of pigs and they set out to confirm it. It was true. The pigs were gone and they found the previously possessed man clothed and in his right mind, sitting at the feet of Jesus listening and learning, filled with love and gratitude, and peaceful for the first time in years. Furthermore, as the story goes, Ari begged Jesus to let him follow him as a disciple, but this prophet Jesus sent him away. He told my friend to go home to his family and to be sure to tell his good news that Jesus delivered him from evil. And Ari did just that! He told everyone in his town about his freedom at the hand of Jesus. Inexplicably, in contrast, the townspeople were afraid of Jesus and begged the miracle worker to leave. *Why were they afraid of Jesus or his power?*

While I was considering these events people started to gather in anticipation of Jesus' arrival in my town with his band of disciples who were following him. I overhead whispers and the tales of people being healed by his touch. That's exactly what I longed for, a kind touch that would heal my suffering.

Could these things be true? Did this Jesus have power over storms and demons? Was he a healer? If so, could I be healed? He wouldn't dare touch me, but could I dare to secretly touch him?

Suddenly he was here, strolling down the gravel path through town, surrounded by a throng of people. It seemed like everyone in town rushed toward Jesus with hope and anticipation that they might catch a glimpse of him or receive a miracle of their own.

As a bystander, beyond the acceptable edge of humanity, I hid in the shadows, my familiar place in the community. I knew my place well, reinforced by twelve years of ruthless reminders. I felt invisible and unworthy to even watch. Yet, the parade of people streaming past me drew me in. I could not stop myself from watching in hope against hope that I too might receive a kind glance, a warm touch, a healing miracle.

I wanted to know if this man was real, to see his face up close and touch him. Other than an accidental graze, an intentional shove, or a doctor's exam, my life lacked a physical connection with another person for over a decade. Can you imagine how painful it is to live like that?

Standing on the edge of the crowd, in my mind, I pictured myself dropping to the ground and crawling in the dust toward Jesus. Before I knew it, my imagination got the best of me and there I was on my hands and knees navigating the dusty maze of sandals and clamoring feet, weaving my way toward Jesus. No one noticed me as I was swept up by the rush of the crowd. I grew captivated by the hope that I might be able to steer myself clear and near enough, just enough, to feel the fringe of his robe. I wasn't afraid of Jesus like the Gerasenes. *If he was real, if he was truly a prophet, if God healed through him...*

Through the dust and despite my stinging watery eyes I saw the sandaled feet which all other sandals followed. A simple but well-worn robe hung down just below his knees. *I can see it, but can I reach it?* I strained my arm past one final obstacle standing between me and my hope. I reached out my hand, stretched my fingers, and, stretching, straining, *Yes!* I touched the hem of his robe. *A warm, powerful current passed through my body. What is this sensation? Am I healed? I only touched the fringe of his robe. Yes, I am whole. I am well.*

It was real; I felt it. He was real; I knew it. Something happened; and He knew it too. The crowd, unaware, nearly trampled me as I knelt humbly and silently in awe of Jesus. But then I heard him speak.

"Who touched me?"

Now I was afraid. I broke the rules. As someone who was considered ceremonially unclean because of my constant bleeding, I was forbidden to have any physical contact with anyone. But I touched a person, and not just any person; I touched the hem of a holy man's robe. I was still crouched in the cloud of dust near his feet when I realized my vulnerable position. As the dust cleared, I saw that I was surrounded by an unfriendly crowd. Caught in a brazen act by Jesus, I could die by any of their hands very shortly, even his.

Amidst a barrage of "I didn't!" and "Not me!" denials, someone spoke to him, "Master, people are crowding and pressing in all around you..."

"Someone touched me," he interrupted. "Power went out from me."

From my knees, I cautiously spoke up.

"It was me. I touched you. I have been ill and untouchable for twelve years," I confessed.

Everyone backed away from me in disgust and held their breath. Some looked for stones. He raised one hand in pause.

"No doctor has been able to help me and I live as an outcast, alone, and in pain. I heard about you and your healing miracles. I thought if I could just touch your robe, I could be healed. Indeed, when I touched the fringe of your garment, I felt your power heal me immediately."

Jesus gently raised my bowed face, looked into my eyes, and with his hands joined to mine, he lifted me to my feet.

"Daughter, your faith has healed you. Go in peace and be freed from your suffering."

Daughter? He called me daughter! He granted me peace. Wait! He touched me. He touched me! HE touched ME!

With His words, His healing power, and His touch, Jesus made me whole. He may have credited this metamorphosis of mine to my faith, but I know He is the true source of the power of my healing.

What a difference a moment can make! I walked away from my brief encounter with Jesus with a healed body and a peaceful spirit. No longer shunned, people welcomed my presence and wanted to hear my story. No longer judged as unclean by the religious laws that guide our people, my community welcomed my fellowship. No longer alienated from my family, I was warmly received back with open arms in what proved to be a painfully sweet reunion after twelve years of separation. My family suffered along with me the whole time, not just from the loss of our relationship but also from religious and social persecution due to their association with me. But that is all behind us now. I am restored.

I share my story with anyone who will listen and even bother the people who don't really care to listen! Afterall, did not the prophet Ezekiel command us to speak to others and tell them whether they listen or not? Just like the disciples who were rescued in the storm, just like my friend Ari who was set free, I tell everyone I meet about the power of God, and about the love and kindness of my Lord Jesus. I want everyone to know what He has done for me, and what He will do for anyone who has the courage and faith to reach out for Jesus.

Explore

- *Psalm 147:4* | God names and numbers the stars.
- *Luke 8:22–25; Matthew 8:23–27* | The disciples lack faith in the middle of a storm.
- *Luke 8:26–39; Matthew 8:28–34* | Jesus frees a man from a legion of demons.
- *Luke 8:38-39* | Jesus is the talk of the town.
- *Luke 8:40* | The whole town wants to see Jesus!
- *Luke 8:43–48* | Twelve years of suffering ended.
- *Mark 5:25–34* | She tells the whole truth.
- *Matthew 9:20–22* | Her faith heals her.
- *Isaiah 55:6* | CARPE DIEM: Seek God when He is near.
- *Leviticus 15:25* | What Law condemns and isolates the woman?
- *Ezekiel 3:11* | Preach, whether people listen or not!

Reflect

- What story does your life tell? Is there an overarching theme?
- How could the power of God frighten some people?
- How might demons or illness destroy relationships with people you care about deeply?
- Is there anything in your life that inhibits relationships?
- What could keep you from reaching out to Jesus?
- What do you want most from Jesus?
- Who is worthy of Jesus' attention?
- What has God given you for which you are grateful?

Imagine

Do you have a "happy place"? Is there someplace where you feel completely safe and at ease? Perhaps it's a familiar place like a sunny beach or a breathtaking mountain top. Or is there a cozy spot where you feel very comfortable? Maybe there's a beautiful place in your imagination where you've always longed to visit.

Take a moment to visualize your happy safe place. See it in your mind's eye in living color, hear the sounds, inhale the air, feel your surroundings, and imagine Jesus is right there with you—because He is.

What are your concerns today? Jesus would like to hear them. He truly cares about you and what concerns you. Maybe one or two specific needs rise above all the others. These are likely your deepest or most pressing concerns. What are they?

As you share your needs with Jesus in prayer, He might ask you if you are placing your faith 100% in Him? That's a pretty big number! It's tempting to hold out a little hope that our friends or family will come to our rescue, and it's all too easy to reserve just a little faith in a clever plan, even if there is only a slim chance it will succeed.

Jesus wants you to know that you don't need to have a ton of faith. You only need faith that is the size of a mustard seed, which is very small (Matthew 17:20–21). Jesus is not concerned about how much faith you have, but where you place your faith—it must be in Jesus, and Him alone. Honestly, if you have enough faith to pray to Jesus, you're doing fine! You already have more than a mustard seed of faith. Plant it and watch it grow!

Jesus invites you to leave your cares and concerns with Him, putting all your faith in Him. Believe that He hears you, He will answer you, and He will address your concerns.

Feel free now to return to your busy place and continue to live the amazing life God has given you knowing that you can check in with Jesus any time. Be sure to return to Him as often as needed whenever you feel these concerns rise to the surface. He is always ready to listen and respond. Make sure you quiet yourself and listen too. Jesus has so much to say to you to encourage you whenever you spend time with Him in your happy safe place.

Cast all your anxiety on him because he cares for you.

1 Peter 5:7 (NIV)

Chapter 12

Out of the Shadows

We Met at the Well

Jesus stood and said in a loud voice,
"Let anyone who is thirsty come to me and drink."

John 7:37b (NIV)

I waited impatiently, sheltered by the cool darkness of the mud brick house I currently called home. My companion surreptitiously slipped out of bed earlier that morning, as he did most days, and left me alone to face the revealing light of dawn and harsh scrutiny of judgmental eyes. I tried, every day, to avoid being seen, but somehow never escaped being noticed. My family and friends shamed and avoided me because of my unfortunate life, as if it might rub off on them. But my difficult life wasn't my fault, or was it? Sadness and loneliness, my constant companions, spoke accusations of blame whenever my mind wandered. I shook my head as if I could dislodge and vanquish them from my mind.

Peeking out from time to time, I waited inside until I verified that the women finished their errands out and about town, at the market, and were back from the well. They eventually returned home to seek refuge from the heat of the day. As they each welcomed relief from the rising sun that scorched the ground and burned their faces, I quietly emerged from the shadows into the bright midday light. My eyes stung from the sun's harsh noon time rays. It seemed that each ensuing year further darkened my soul and contrastingly brightened the days. Just as my aging eyes struggled to adapt to the visual change from darkness to light, my spirit struggled to accept the painful contrast of the life I planned and the life I lived.

I entered the world as we all do, with hope. My loving parents nurtured me as their firstborn in Sychar, a Samaritan town formerly known as Shechem. Centuries ago, when Moses led our people out of bondage in Egypt and the tribes completed their meandering sojourn in the wilderness, Joshua buried the bones of Joseph here in our town. This promised land of Canaan offered freedom for us to worship God and live as an independent people and nation under His kingship. Prior to the exodus and reaching further backwards in time before our people found refuge in Egypt, our forefather Jacob dug a well here in Shechem and built an altar to honor the Lord. Even before that, the patriarch Abram traveled from Ur and then Haran to settle here with his wife with hope and a promise from God to start a family of their own. This enduring legacy of Shechem is ever-present in my hometown called Sychar.

I was told that the day I emerged from the safety of my mother's womb included rejoicing and promises of a bright future. Having approached fifty years of age, my hope faded with each passing sunset; each sunrise illuminated the reality of my life. I have not known the loving kindness of a faithful husband, nor have I known the joys of a child to call me Eema, or Mother. Misfortune and poor choices have filled the chapters of my life. Honestly, maybe my choices were rooted in my plight as an orphan looking for safety in the home of a man who might help me recapture my lost sense of family and belonging.

First century Samaria bred a community and a lifestyle of harsh contradictions. Sychar, my hometown, lay in the valley between Mount Gerizim and Mount Ebal, locations that memorialized the benefits and penalties of life in the promised land. Moses commanded the Hebrews to hold the Ceremony of Blessings and Curses here after they entered the Promised Land. While half the people stood on Mount Gerizim to recite the blessings of God, the other half countered from Mount Ebal with penalties for living contrary to God's ways. The mountains themselves stood as constant and stark reminders that God watches His people.

Unfortunately, the land of promise proved a struggle during much of the nearly 2,000 or so years my people lived here so far. Certainly, life in Sychar, Samaria included blessings, but it also included curses.

I, myself, embodied contradictions. My name Dinah means "vindicated" as if from birth I was meant to carry the approval of God throughout my life. However, my name also means "judged," and I carried the weight of that sort of disapproval from my community daily. Why was I named Dinah? No one could tell me. What's in a name anyway? It's just a name. But names have a way of sticking, lingering in mind, and even defining a life.

I often thought of the other Dinah, the daughter of Jacob, who dug our well. I wondered about the young prince, Shechem, who lived in the town that bore his name. After her family's arrival in the valley, he saw young Dinah out and about, desired her, and despite her forceful objections, assaulted and raped her. Although he claimed to love her and schemed to marry her, Dinah's brothers set out to punish him for what he did to their baby sister.

They deceitfully plotted revenge upon Shechem and all the men of his tribe. Two of her brothers killed every male in the city, and the rest joined together and plundered the wealth and people in every household. Though they rescued Dinah and brought her home, nothing could restore what she lost. Rescue is not the same as restoration.

Though meant to be a place of freedom, hope and worship, Shechem was also remembered as a place of betrayal, revenge, sexual assault, and murder. My city had a long history and an even longer memory. Historical Shechem and my ancient sister Dinah reminded me that in my town Sychar, I too lived in a state of vulnerability.

Finally leaving home near high noon with my empty water jug, I turned my thoughts back to the immediate task. As I approached Jacob's well, I noticed a man seated on the edge. I knew most everyone in the valley, but I did not recognize him.

Is he lost?

My steps faltered momentarily. *He's a Jew.*

I paused. *Am I safe?*

Centuries of animosity between us Samaritans and the Jews created a rift so wide we generally refused to have anything to do with each other. *Why should I give up my errand, this is my well, not this stranger's!* I cautiously approached without making eye contact.

"Will you give me a drink?" he asked politely.

I stiffened and answered defensively, "You are a Jew, and I am a Samaritan woman. How can you ask me for a drink?" I suspected his words and potential actions might be a trap.

"If you knew the gift of God and who it is that asks you for a drink, you would have asked him, and he would have given you living water."

I was confused by the way the stranger turned his request for a drink of water back to me, as if I was the one who asked for water. I argued back, "You have nothing to draw with and the well is deep. Where can you get this living water? Are you greater than our father Jacob, who gave us the well and drank from it himself?"

He gestured toward the well.

"Everyone who drinks this water will be thirsty again. But whoever drinks the water I give them will never thirst. The water I give will become in them a spring of water welling up to eternal life."

I thoughtfully whispered his words to myself; *never thirst, never thirst again.* I imagined what it would be like if I did not have to trek back and forth from my home day after day for the life-sustaining water from the well. *Never thirst again!*

I answered searchingly, "Sir, give me this water so that I won't get thirsty and have to keep coming here to draw water." It no longer mattered to me that he was a man, or a Jew. This seemed like my lucky break! I had no idea my encounter was so much more than that. Unaware, I stood at the threshold of a unique destiny prepared for me from before the beginning of time.

Suddenly the conversation seemed to take a wrong turn.

"Go, call your husband and come back," he requested.

"I have no husband," I replied with embarrassment.

"You are right when you say you have no husband. The fact is, you have had five husbands, and the man you now have is not your husband. What you have just said is quite true."

Wow! How did we quickly go from talking about water and thirst to such an uncomfortable and personal confrontation? I inhaled slowly as the names of my six men passed through my mind. While most of them probably started with good intentions, intentions didn't go very far in the real world. Unlike Dinah of ancient Shechem who had six brothers who did what they thought best and fought for their only sister, the men in my life did not seem so inclined. *But this man seems quite different. Kind. Caring. And he knows things, things about me. How?* An awkward silence concealed my internal reflections.

"I can see that you are a prophet," I finally asserted. "Our ancestors worshiped on this mountain, but you Jews claim that the place where we must worship is in Jerusalem."

Maybe I can deflect his attention away from me and my place of vulnerability, my failed family life. Can I steer the conversation to a mere discussion of religion, perhaps his area of expertise? Am I throwing darts at whatever pops up? Maybe I'm not used to conversing with an honest and sincere man. Maybe...

"Believe me," he interrupted my thoughts, "a time is coming when you will worship the Father neither on this mountain nor in Jerusalem. A time is coming, and has now come, when the true worshipers will worship the Father in the Spirit and in truth, for they are the kind of worshipers the Father seeks. God is spirit, and his worshipers must worship in the Spirit and in truth."

Whoa! Am I discussing deep theology with a Jewish man sitting on the edge of a well in broad daylight at noon? Is he saying it's not about where we worship, but rather how we worship? This goes against everything I have been taught about worship on these mountains. What does it mean to worship in Spirit and in truth?

"Well, I know that Messiah is coming. When he comes, he will explain everything to us." And with that final word, I decided to end the conversation. But he continued, "I, the one speaking to you—I am He."

I stared without blinking, stunned by what the man said. I never expected to hear anything like this. My mind swirled as I repeated his words, *"The one speaking to you...I am He."*

Could this man be the long-awaited holy one of God? Was this man the one who would bring justice and mercy to the world—to my world?

At that moment, I believed. Standing there in the heat of the day at a crossroads of faith, I finally found someone worth believing. Not because he was a good and kind man but because he was much more than a man—he was the Messiah!

I need to tell somebody. Anybody. Everybody!

I bolted away, leaving behind both my water jug and my Messiah. I hurried back into town.

"Come quickly!" I shouted. "I met the Prophet of God at Jacob's well. He told me everything I ever did!"

Those who knew me were skeptical that an outsider knew anything about me. But, intrigued by my frantic fervor, people hastened out to see if my story had any substance. Besides, in my hurry, I didn't even ask the man his name.

The people arrived to find the man, who called himself, "Jesus," just as I said. My water jug sat beside the well, filled to the brim with cool fresh life-giving water.

Thus ensued a banter of intense questioning and answers from both sides. Before long, many of the townspeople agreed with me—Jesus not only appeared to be a prophet, but the long-awaited Messiah. Excitedly, we all urged him, along with some of his disciples who had arrived, to join us in Sychar to talk further about the kingdom of God. We Samaritans demonstrated a great thirst for knowledge about the scriptures and the incredible possibility that Jesus could be the promised Messiah. It seemed everyone wanted the living water of eternal life that he promised to all who believe in him.

Jesus graciously accepted our offer to linger a while longer with us so we could know him better. As he continued his teaching, many in my community believed in him as the Messiah. His words helped break through our fortified walls of distrust between us and gently opened doors of faith.

Many of us marveled that God cared so much that he came to find us in our own small town in Samaria. Men, women, and children alike followed my act of faith as they believed in Jesus. Not only that, but after two days with Jesus and the disciples, people approached me with deep gratitude.

"We no longer believe just because of what you said, now we have heard for ourselves, and we know that this man really is the Savior of the world."

Jesus moved on shortly thereafter with his disciples to seek others with a hunger and thirst for God. I soon found myself enjoying profound blessings that resulted from my choice to worship Jesus as Messiah and shamelessly bring others—even those who shamed me for years—to meet and know Him, too.

I no longer hid in spiritual and physical darkness. I stopped avoiding light. Former condemning voices showered me with appreciation and praise. I rejoiced in open fellowship with God and worshiped in hope and wonder with my neighbors.

Each new sunrise opened the door to bright expectations for me and every sunset marked the peaceful close of a day of restoration. Jesus gave me forgiveness, belonging, dignity, and love such as I had never known. I learned to embrace the truth and live as the prophet of Isaiah encouraged, "Come, descendants of Jacob, let us walk in the light of the Lord."

The beloved apostle John who I also met that wonderful day at Jacob's well, preserved my story in his writings. *Perhaps he thought it was important for people to know that the first person to whom Jesus revealed His true identity was me, an unlikely Samaritan woman one dusty day at Jacob's well!*

John wrote in one of his letters, "But if we walk in the light, as he is in the light, we have fellowship with one another, and the blood of Jesus, his Son, purifies us from all sin." *These words of the apostle John echoed the patriarch Jacob. They both urged us to step out into the light of the Lord. Be unashamed in Him! Believe in Jesus as Messiah and enjoy the fellowship of the family of God that endures forever.*

Explore

- *John 4:1–42* | HIGH NOON at the Well in Sychar, Samaria.

- *Genesis 12:1, 6* | Shechem is an ancient city that existed in 2000 B.C.

- *John 4:4–6* | Sychar and ancient Shechem are the same town. Jacob's well is there.

- *Deuteronomy 11:29* | You will stand on Mount Gerizim and Mount Ebal one day.

- *Deuteronomy 27 and 28* | You will recite the blessings and the curses of your choices.

- *Joshua 8:30–34* | Half the people at Mount Gerizim and half in front of Mount Ebal.

- *Genesis 12:6–7 and 33:19* | Abram and Jacob both made an altar to God in Shechem.

- *Genesis 30:20–21* | Dinah of ancient Shechem had six older brothers.

- *Genesis 34:25–26* | Dinah of ancient Shechem was rescued by her brothers.

- *John 4:18* | Dinah of Sychar, Samaria had six men in her life.

- *Matthew 5:6* | Some people are hungry and thirsty.

- *Isaiah 2:5* | Walk in the light.

- *1 John 1:7* | Keep walking in the light.

- *Deuteronomy 31:8* | God will never abandon you.

Reflect

- How do you think Dinah of ancient Shechem felt when her brothers rescued her?

- Does Dinah of ancient Shechem tell us something about shame and redemption?

- How would you describe the hesitancy Dinah of Sychar felt as she encountered a man at Jacob's well?

- Why do you think Dinah of Sychar was willing to believe in Jesus?

- What would Dinah of Sychar say about shame and redemption?

- Is it possible that Jesus was thinking of Dinah of ancient Shechem when He sat down at Jacob's well in Sychar?

- If so, how might Jesus' memory of Dinah of ancient Shechem have influenced His interaction with Dinah of Sychar?

Imagine

Can you picture yourself inside on a very hot day? It's cool and dark inside with all the windows and shades closed. But you are thirsty, and desperate to go out to the well for a jug of cool fresh water. When you finally emerge at noon, no one sees you. Everyone has already been to the well and returned home with their refreshment. You carry your empty water jug in one hand and shade your eyes with the other. As you blink in the bright sun, it looks like there is someone seated on the edge of the well. Getting closer you can see there is someone at the well, and it is Jesus. He told His disciples that He had to go through Samaria, and He stopped at Jacob's well. He is waiting there for you. He is looking forward to seeing you. You are the one He wanted to see.

Jesus greets you with a kind smile and wants to know how you are doing? He asks you if there is any part of you that feels as empty as your water jug? Talk with Jesus and tell Him how you are feeling. Confide in Him and trust Him with your truth. He is listening closely. He can handle it.

While you have been talking with Jesus, you notice He has been gradually filling your empty water jug with life-giving water. He has been refreshing you and filling your soul with His Spirit. Turning to go you tell Jesus that even if you don't have to return to the well every day, that you will come back daily, to meet with Him and enjoy His company.

Jesus is delighted that you would choose to spend time with Him, just as He chose to spend time with you. "I am looking forward to seeing you again," He calls to you. Could anything keep you from returning often to drink from the well of living water that you find in Jesus? He is waiting for you.

I will give water to the one who thirsts
from the spring of the water of life.

Revelation 21:6b (NASB)

Chapter 13

A Reversal of Fortune

Abigail's Reward

One who walks blamelessly will receive help,
but one who is crooked will fall all at once.

Proverbs 28:18 (NASB)

T he wilderness had become home for David, the one-time shepherd, and now famous warrior. His tents were always moving, or so it seemed, and caves were a frequent refuge as needed. David roamed the land of promise while waiting for the realization of his own. Though anointed as the future king of the Hebrew nation, he was on the run, fleeing from the man who currently occupied the throne, Saul.

At one time, the king loved David as much as a father would love a son, if not more. In addition to marrying his daughter and serving in Saul's personal military detail, David helped soothe Saul's tormented mind and refresh his spirit, skillfully playing the harp and singing inspired words that sounded like prayers.

But all that changed when King Saul veered away from faithful obedience to God. In response, the Almighty removed His blessing from the man He selected to lead His nation and

125

quietly appointed David as Saul's successor with his anointing by the prophet Samuel. Whereas Saul once loved David, his bitterness and rage turned him against his son-in-law and unintended protégé. His evil antics drove David from Saul's palace to seek safety elsewhere.

David, on the other hand, loved Saul's family and considered it illegal, imprudent, and ungodly to threaten the king or anyone else in the royal family. Saul did not return the favor. Instead, he repeatedly terrorized David and anyone who associated with him. His paranoia led him to attempt to kill his own son, Jonathan, because he suspected he was conspiring against him with David. Jonathan and David shared a covenant of brotherly friendship that frightened King Saul.

David's tenuous existence and abrupt departure from the royal family separated him from his wife, Michal. Before long, the wilderness entourage included two new wives to manage David's tents, Ahinoam and Abigail. Although from different regions and tribes, they had one thing in common: David. Oh, those eyes! He was indeed handsome. His eyes—along with his muscular build and velvety voice—melted hearts.

Ahinoam hailed from Jezreel. David chose her for reasons known only to him, but her hometown offers a clue. Perched on a hillside overlooking a wide valley, Jezreel sat in a natural strategic location. Ahinoam may have been a trophy from a military conquest and a symbol of David's strength. Their marriage may have provided an alliance with the regional inhabitants and helped keep David safe while traversing that area of the country. Whatever the reason, she settled into her new life, made the best of it, and they welcomed a son.

Abigail added extraordinary beauty and intelligence to David's inner circle. Before she met the future king on the run, she wisely and fairly managed the household of her very wealthy, but mean and surly, husband, Nabal.

Now that Ahinoam and Abigail were married to the same man, they spent a lot of time together while he sought to avoid capture by Saul, pursued the enemies of God, and waited for his time to lead the fledgling nation. Ahinoam wanted to know more of Abigail's story. Perhaps the details were pleasant, or painful, but if they were going to live together she wanted to know her better. David was gone all the time anyway, so they might as well be friends.

She finally inquired one afternoon, "Abigail, what is your story? Where are you from and how did you get here?"

Abigail wanted to know Ahinoam better, too, and sharing their stories offered ample opportunity. Though she preferred to forget the past, important life lessons deserved retelling. She considered her life a profound narrative about God, how He showed up in a desperate moment, and turned the heart of a man away from avoidable vengeance. Beyond all the chaotic events of Abigail's story, one thing was clear—God protected and provided for her and her household.

"My husband before David," she began, "Nabal, was very wealthy by most standards. We had 1,000 goats and 3,000 sheep, much more than we needed."

Ahinoam nodded. "That's a lot of wool!"

"But sadly, Nabal gained much more wealth than wisdom. He foolishly lacked appreciation for the abundance of God's blessings in our lives. He also lacked caution, and recklessly almost cost many of us our lives."

Ahinoam knew some of this part, but she had never heard it from Abigail's perspective.

"David and 600 warriors camped in the fields where Nabal kept our flocks of sheep. As a former shepherd himself, David and his men protected our flocks and befriended our shepherds. They were good to our shepherds, helped keep everyone safe, and we lost nothing that whole season.

"David stood tall in our hearts and minds. We heard tales of his various exploits and battlefield victories, stories about him killing bears and lions while shepherding his own family flocks, and, of course, how he killed the giant enemy of God and our people—Goliath. Jesse's youngest son was famous for many reasons before we met him, and he deserved respect.

"When Nabal brought the sheep to Carmel for shearing that year, David sent ten young men to join in the festivities and to request the rightful compensation for the protections they provided. I wasn't there, but our servants quickly told me what happened."

She shook her head sadly at the memory.

"David's men first greeted Nabal saying, 'Have a long life, peace to you Nabal, your household, and all that you have. We have protected your flock and your shepherds these many months, and now we humbly ask for whatever you choose to spare to show your appreciation for us and for David.' However, Nabal responded with insults, acted like he didn't know anything about David or the good services the men had provided, and sent them away empty handed.

"Fortunately, one of our servants came privately and told me what Nabal said and did. To say my husband's behavior alarmed me is an understatement; I was terrified for Nabal, me, and our entire household. My fear proved genuine when we heard David and 400 fierce men were headed our way to execute justice, or revenge, upon our tribe. I was used to dealing shrewdly with Nabal's wickedness, knew better than to confront him, and knew time was of the essence. I trusted God and acted quickly to try and prevent a disaster."

Her voice shook and the muscles in her face and neck visibly tightened as she recounted the traumatic event.

"I directed my household to gather bread, wine, grain, raisins, figs, and sheep prepared for roasting. We loaded up the donkeys and I sent servants with the provisions ahead of me to meet David on his way. Then I put on my finest robes and jewelry, anointed my face with perfumed oil, and rode out to intervene before they reached our tents.

"As I entered a ravine, I observed David and his men descending the mountainside toward me. As we met on the path, I dismounted from my mule and bowed as low to the ground as possible. I offered my greetings and apologized for my husband's folly and the dishonor heaped upon them. I suggested I deserved the blame for not knowing about their request and begged for our lives. I appealed to his honor and integrity, reminded him of his future, and explained that I hoped to spare him grief or a troubled heart if someday, as king, he remembered this terrible day when he went ahead of God and took revenge for himself. I had in mind the Song of Moses when God asserted His right to vindicate His people, take vengeance on His adversaries, and repay those who hate Him.

"David patiently allowed me to complete my appeal. In the silence that followed, I prayed that my husband's wicked folly and foolishness would not result in needless, reactionary retaliation. I almost couldn't believe it when David smiled and shouted, 'Bless the Lord! He sent you to spare me from doing evil. And bless you, Abigail, for your discernment. If you had not come to me so quickly, my anger and hastiness would have led me to destroy Nabal and all the men of his tribe. Go now, and return to your home in peace, the same peace I originally offered to Nabal.' He accepted the provisions I offered, and my apology, and turned back from his intended actions.

"That evening, Nabal hosted a feast fit for a king to celebrate the sheep shearing. He behaved like a drunken fool and I didn't dare risk telling him what happened. The next morning, when I did tell him and detailed how close he came to death and destruction, his body seized up in fear. I don't know if he was able to reflect on his behavior or seek any forgiveness for his life choices, but he died ten days later."

The two women sat quietly in the shared shadow of stark reality and near disaster. Abigail sighed deeply and continued.

"Shortly thereafter, David sent messengers to Carmel with a marriage proposal. As the widow of a foolish, wealthy man with a large enterprise, I leaped at the opportunity for many reasons. I departed quickly with five of my maidens and here we are. My life is much different now, as we both know."

That evening, resting her head on a straw cushion, Ahinoam reflected on Abigail's account. She clearly saw God at work in Abigail's life. She marveled at Abigail's courage and successful reaction in the face of dire circumstances. She, too, admired Abigail's wisdom.

May the Lord grant me wisdom to know when to act quickly and when to wait. What a blessing to share life with a woman so filled with the knowledge of God and the courage to live according to God's ways.

Explore

- *1 Samuel 25* | How it all goes down between David, Abigail and Nabal.

- *1 Samuel 15:11* | God regrets making Saul the King.

- *1 Samuel 16:12* | David has beautiful eyes (NASB) that "sparkle" (CEV).

- *1 Samuel 16:7, 11–13, 18* | David: Musician and Warrior.

- *1 Samuel 25:3* | Abigail: Intelligent and Beautiful.

- *1 Samuel 25:25* | Nabal: Worthless and Stupid (NASB).

- *1 Samuel 25:43* | Ahinoam: Unremarkable.

- *1 Samuel 17–24* | THE RISE AND FALL of DAVID: from most favored to most hated.

- *Deuteronomy 32:35* | Leave vengeance to God.

- *1 Chronicles 3:1* | David's firstborn son is with Ahinoam, second born son is with Abigail.

Reflect

- Where does God fit into the story of your life?

- Abigail acted quickly to plead for mercy from David, and she acted quickly to accept David's proposal of marriage. She was praised for her quick action. When is a quick response the best course of action?

- David nearly acted too quickly to exact revenge upon Nabal before Abigail stopped him from making a mistake that he would have likely regretted. When is it better to delay a response?

- When does action matter most? When does waiting matter most?

- Both Nabal and Abigail experienced a reversal of fortune. How might a reversal of fortune be for the best?

- David was waiting in the wilderness for his time to become king. What does waiting in the wilderness mean to you?

Imagine

Everyone agrees, it's going to be a wonderful reunion for the family of God as we all come together to honor our Heavenly Father. Can you picture yourself at this celebration? Throngs of people have assembled ready to share their tales of the goodness of God. Tonight, it's all about Him. Having endured so many sarcastic roasts of our friends, and survived the braggadocios speeches by our co-workers, it will be refreshing to share sweet stories of our Father. The possibilities are infinite. How can anyone choose which story to tell?

What life story would you chose to tell about how much our Heavenly Father means to you? Don't worry, it isn't your turn yet. We're going to be here a while, a long while! Take time to reflect. Look for the evidence that God has been with you and watching over you. The proof is there, though it may require some humility and honesty to see it. Have you ever experienced an inexplicable peace amid life's storms? Have you had supernatural courage in the face of danger or illness? Have you been blessed in ways that you could never have achieved on your own? You have many gifts and talents that honor your Heavenly Father, gifted to you at birth. Perhaps a timeline of your life, thus far, will open your eyes to how many times our Heavenly Father has shown up for you.

Ask God to reveal to you how He has loved you and been a part of your life thus far. Consider writing a short speech to express your appreciation at the heavenly family reunion. You may want to stick your speech in your pocket and carry it with you to remind yourself that, when things get tough, your Heavenly Father loves you and will stick with you. It will also be a nice reminder to say, "Thank you Father!" when things are going incredibly well. No matter what the circumstances, nothing can break the ties that bind us together in the family of God.

For this reason I kneel before the Father,
from whom every family in heaven
and on earth derives its name.

Ephesians 3:14–15 (NIV)

Dear Diary

Mary of Magdala's Confession

Would God not find this out?
For He knows the secrets of the heart.

Psalm 44:21 (NASB)

I t happened again. I feel frustrated and misunderstood. How can it be, that Jesus is the only one who truly knows me and knows the truth about me? People make assumptions and jump to conclusions, and in so doing, forget the truth about me.

But you, secret Diary, you know me, right? You do know who I am? Or do you, like most everyone else, think I was a prostitute, before I met Jesus? What a lie! It hurts to know that so many people think that of me. The truth is painful enough without adding terrible accusations that are not true. I was not a prostitute before I met Jesus!

Dear Diary, my silent friend, like so many others, do you have other untrue beliefs about me? Do you think that I was the sinful woman who washed Jesus' feet with her tears at the house of the Pharisee, Simon? Did I wipe his feet with my long hair and anoint them with oil? No, that was not me either!

Oh, how people build hollow narratives with certainty and conviction. With no evidence but unvetted assertions, they commit to whole untruths. I was not the woman at the home of Simon the Pharisee's who washed Jesus' feet with her tears!

People's lies about me distort the truth. I remember Jesus teaching that the devil "is a liar and the father of lies." So, of course, the devil would seek to spread false stories about me; anything to prevent telling true stories about Jesus.

So, Dear Diary, one last time, I offer a final challenge if you want to truly know me. This is my story.

When Jesus first began to preach and heal the sick, people were curious about him. One such man, a Pharisee named Simon, invited Jesus to dinner in his home. A woman, known as a prostitute, entered the Pharisee's home uninvited and washed Jesus' feet in a humble act of repentance. No one knew her name but her story of forgiveness spread far and wide. For the record, dear Diary, I am not that woman.

When Jesus and his followers went to the city of Bethany last week, just prior to Passover, a woman named Mary (yes, we are both named "Mary") anointed Jesus' feet with costly perfume. John, the beloved disciple, knows what happened and recorded it in notes he has been keeping about Jesus.

As he rightly notes, Mary of Bethany was the one who anointed Jesus that day. Martha was serving us at the home of Simon the Leper, and her sister Mary demonstrated her love for Jesus in that beautiful act of worship. But, Dear Diary, I am not that Mary.

My earliest memory recalls me sitting in my mother's lap surrounded by my seven older brothers and sisters in our family home in Magdala. We listen intently to the deep, warm voice of our father teaching us from the holy scriptures because he believes in the wisdom of Proverbs: "Train a child in the way he (should) go; and even when old, he will not swerve from it."

My father looks serious, yet kind. He holds high hopes for all his children. He believes we each have a destiny and an important future. He speaks of seven things God hates, and I see these words and phrases as dark clouds above our heads:

"A haughty look,
   A lying tongue,
Hands that shed innocent blood,
   A heart that plots wicked schemes,
Feet swift in running to do evil,
   A false witness who lies with every breath,
And him who sows strife among brothers."

The Torah is filled with real people who fell victim to these deadly sins. My father looks intently, locking his gaze on ours, each in turn before firmly warning, "Run from the seven things that Adonai hates." He believes we can choose to live a holy life dedicated to God. With all my heart I want to run from everything that God hates; I want to run to God!

Dear Diary, I also remember myself older—alone and in pain, suffering from an affliction of mind and soul. At this point in my divergent life, I act like a wild animal. I strike out at every hand extended in charity and compassion. I drive everyone away, as if somehow driving people away will drive out the demons.

Seven have captured and possess me like cruel masters. One for every day of the week, perhaps, and I am never free of their torment. They tell me what to do, and I am helplessly bound under their control.

Yes, my father taught me to choose a life of holy devotion to God and to avoid the seven things that God hates. I expect he never dreamed that demons could overtake his daughter and prevent her from living such a life. I wish I could forget those painful memories, but their memories remind me how desperately I needed deliverance, as well as who delivered me and set me free.

Dear Diary, I remember that day, yes, that glorious day that Jesus of Nazareth arrived in the town where I grew up and still lived, Magdala. In the scrapbook of my mind, Jesus, the rabbi, stands there bright and beautiful. He lingers, teaching on the shore of the Sea of Galilee. Though surrounded by a crowd, he takes time for everyone. He listens, he cares, and he cures. He touches people, he speaks, and miracles happen right in front of us.

At one point, he sees me. Yet, instead of abandoning me to the evil whims of my possessive horde, Jesus moves toward me with compassion. Though the seven evil spirits attempt to push him away and screech, he is neither deterred nor overpowered. He speaks to them and they to him as if they know each other, and they immediately obey his command to exit my life as if they must.

At first, I hear nothing. Silence fills the space vacated only moments ago. I finally recognize silence, my old friend from whom I have not heard in such a long time. My life has been very noisy, unrelentingly so, for much too long. Then, I hear the quiet voice of Jesus.

"Mary. Mary of Magdala. Your demons are banished. You are free."

He reaches out his hand and lifts me from where I have fallen. I hardly remember the last time I felt a gentle touch.

He asks, "Follow me?"

I think Jesus usually speaks commandingly. But I also think that perhaps he knows more about my state of mind than I do, and he acts accordingly with tenderness.

I feel free, and realize with unquestionable certainty that, yes, I am free, and I am free to choose. And choose I do.

I choose to follow Jesus.

Dear Diary, as you know, numerous images—like miniature portraits capturing highlight moments in my new life—are beginning to line the pathways of my mind. There I am following Jesus. Here are snapshots of me listening to his teaching. Each bears captions of His words sinking deep into my mind and soul. My mind is healing as these new images mark my journey of peace and restoration to a life of godly action, intent, and purpose.

In these images I see myself serving alongside other followers of Jesus. The healed has become the Healer's helper helping other needy people, and I feel joy.

There I am with other women (some also named "Mary"), gathering our modest financial means and contributing to the preaching of the gospel. We look fulfilled. I know we feel a godly sense of pride in our work, yet with great humility that Jesus called us to share in His ministry of good news!

Whenever Jesus speaks my name, I feel loved. No one has ever said, "Mary," the way Jesus does. He knows me—Mary of Magdala—and the truth about me. He loves me. And I know Jesus and the truth about him. I am eternally devoted to Him.

Dear Diary, you guard my private thoughts and keep them safe under lock and key. You know I seek truth. As Jesus said, "I am the truth," and so it is with all my heart that I follow Jesus. His truth has indeed set me free.

If necessary, let my name fade from the pages of time and history. But, if not, know this: I know Jesus, Jesus knows me, and Jesus knows my story. I am Mary of Magdala.

Explore

- *Luke 7:36–38* | At the home of Simon the Pharisee, an unnamed woman from town washes Jesus' feet.

- *John 12:1–8* | In Bethany, Mary of Bethany washes Jesus' feet.

- *John 8:44* | Who is the father of lies?

- *Proverbs 22:6* | Start the children off well.

- *Proverbs 6:16–19* | GOD HATES SEVEN THINGS!

- *Mark 16:9; Luke 8:2* | SEVEN demons oppressed Mary of Magdala.

- *John 14:6* | Who is the Way, the Truth, and the Life?

- *John 8:32* | The Truth will set you free.

- *John 8:36* | Free indeed!

Reflect

- How would you feel if you heard Jesus say your name?

- What lies does the devil say about you? What lies have you believed?

- What truth does Jesus say about you? How do you know?

Imagine

Do you keep a diary? There was a time when lots of people kept a small book with a lock and key that guarded their secret thoughts. But there was always the risk that someone would find it and break into it. Nowadays some of us keep a safer version, a digital diary. But that is still vulnerable to exposure. For those who say they do not keep a diary, just remember, our minds are automatically keeping track of everything for us in a virtual diary that we call memories.

What if you found out that our heavenly Father has been keeping a journal about you? What if you could compare His journal notes with your diary? Would they align with one another? Or would there be some major differences? Let's imagine that we can break into God's journal, the one He has been keeping on you. What will we discover?

Do you have diary comments complaining that God is not listening to your prayers? God's journal notes say repeatedly that He hears your prayers, all of them (Psalm 55:17). Are there other entries in your diary that say that you feel like God has forgotten you? God's note says that He engraved you on the palms of His hands. He is constantly thinking of you (Isaiah 49:16). Was there ever a sad day where your entry said that you felt worthless? God's note says that you are very precious to Him (Isaiah 43:4). Have you ever confided in your life's diary that you fear that God doesn't love you anymore? Flipping through God's journal, page after page, it says emphatically that His love for you stands firm forever (Psalm 89:2).

These are some major differences! If God is telling the truth, then someone has been telling you lies; lies about yourself and about your heavenly Father. Worse yet, you have believed some of those lies and missed out on the peace and joy that God desires for you.

Perhaps it's time to find the white-out and make some corrections to your thinking. We might even need to pull out some pages and start over. Embrace the truth about yourself in God's eyes and accept God's version about how important you are to God and how He truly feels about you. Reading the Bible every day will speak this truth into your heart and mind and your thoughts will gradually begin to more closely reflect the truth about how much God loves you and is always there for you.

God hears your prayers; He has never forgotten about you and is constantly thinking of you; you are precious to God; and you are loved by Him, today and every day from now until forever. What will be the first entry of your new diary?

Rejoice that your names are written in heaven.

Luke 10:20b (NIV)

Chapter 15

The Magdalene

Mary's Epiphany

It is He who reveals the profound and hidden things;
He knows what is in the darkness,
And the light dwells with Him.

Daniel 2:22 (NASB)

I t was like a dream. A bad dream. Truly a nightmare. How could a dream come true turn into a living hell so quickly? I felt distraught; my heart shattered into a thousand pieces. Jesus found me on the shore of the Sea of Galilee and rescued me from seven demons who ravaged my soul and stole my life away. From that day on, I followed Jesus with a pure and wholehearted devotion, knowing love and forgiveness, peace, and healing for the first time in my life. Now, somehow dark forces had taken revenge on Jesus and stolen his life with the brutal hand of a Roman crucifixion.

I and others who loved and followed Jesus mourned his death as one. We gathered in Jerusalem praying and eating together on the Sabbath. The day stretched endlessly and, yet, we found comfort together, remembering the past three years and miracles that we experienced.

We believed in Jesus as the Messiah, the promised Holy One of God. We followed him and sought to learn from him. We expected him to end the filthy occupation of the Romans, lead the anticipated Day of the Lord, usher in the Kingdom of God, and take his rightful place on the throne of heaven and earth. In his absence, we discussed his great love for us, as well as our struggles to make sense of his teaching. Intermittent relief from our horror and distress only came with fitful sleep as darkness wrapped our fellowship in quiet isolation.

Very early the next morning, I urged the women to help prepare burial spices and go with me to the tomb to finish fulfilling Jewish burial requirements. We went through the motions as if in a trance, still unsure and unable to make sense of what happened. We fought back tears, as well as creeping doubts. We all watched Jesus die and saw where the men placed his body in a burial tomb guarded by Roman soldiers.

In the dim morning light, we carried our spices and silently approached the tomb. Suddenly, the earth shook violently and the massive stone covering the tomb where they laid Jesus' body rolled back to expose the entrance. We dropped our spice jars and clung to one another. While we sought to gather our wits, two brightly gleaming men appeared, and we fearfully bowed our faces to the ground.

"Why do you seek the living One among the dead?" one man, who looked like an angel, asked. "He is not here, but He has risen. Remember how He told you while He was still with you: The Son of Man must be delivered over to the hands of sinners, be crucified, and on the third day be raised again."

We remembered, but it didn't make sense, until now. As if waking from a dream, the women with me arose to turn and hurry back and tell the others who were all still mourning the death of Jesus, along with their fading hopes and dreams, and this was incredibly amazing, unbelievably good news!

I lingered a moment longer. While searching the empty tomb and crying, someone asked me, "Woman, why are you crying? Who is it you are looking for?"

I thought maybe it was the gardener.

"Sir, if you have carried him away, tell me where you have put him and I will get him."

"Mary."

I knew that voice. His voice.

"Mary of Magdala."

I looked up to see Him. Jesus was alive!

"Do not be afraid," he said. "Go and take word to My brethren to leave for Galilee, and there they shall see Me."

When we reached the home where everyone was gathered, we were so excited that we were all talking at once trying to describe what we saw and heard. In response to our strange words, most everyone thought we were crazy. I stood in the doorway watching our friends and fellow disciples begin to argue, shout, and make cynical comments.

As the morning sun radiated brightly behind me, framing my silhouette, I shouted to everyone, "I have seen the Lord! Yes, He is alive!!"

The gathering quieted some, and the other women joined in to confirm that, yes, we all agreed on what we saw and what the angels said. But most still refused to believe us, called our testimony nonsense, attributed our experience to stress or trivial imagination, and cruelly mocked us.

Doubt and fear threatened to overtake me as I recognized familiar tones of taunting, mockery, and shaming. But Jesus' earlier voice prevailed, "Remember." I remembered Him calling me by name, "Mary." I remembered His words of courage, forgiveness, hope, and love. I remembered His gift of freedom from seven demons who terrorized me, and others through me. I remembered, "Do not be afraid." I knew my place, my truth, my Savior and my King. I stood taller, raised my chin and shoulders and calmly repeated, "Jesus is alive."

My self-assured demeanor seemed to break through to Peter and John, the beloved disciple. They both ran past me, Peter first and then John, but John reached the tomb first, which they found empty except for linen and the burial cloth formerly wrapped around Jesus' head. They found exactly what we told them we saw—the tomb where they laid Jesus empty—but even then they had a hard time comprehending it.

Later that day, Jesus appeared to two disciples walking on the road to Emmaus. He appeared to the eleven apostles while they were eating together some days later. At one point, he appeared to more than 500 people at the same time. Along the way, all the disciples began to come to terms with their doubts and disbelief. Jesus was, indeed, crucified, dead, and buried, But, now he was alive, again. He defeated death!

We remembered that when Jesus walked with us before, he referred to the sign of Jonah, who emerged from the belly of a huge fish after three days. Now, we began to understand what Jesus foretold and how that corresponded to him rising from the dead and the grave on the third day.

Jesus rightly scolded those who did not believe our first eyewitness report. He chastised their hard-heartedness. But He also forgave their fear and betrayal, even Peter's. In time, with repentance, prayer, and the gift of His Holy Spirit, we each experienced our own epiphany as we listened, learned, worshiped in spirit and truth, and obeyed his commands.

Explore

- *Matthew 28:1–10* | The Magdalene goes to the tomb and finds that Jesus has risen!

- *Mark 16:1–18* | The Magdalene goes to the tomb and finds that Jesus has risen!

- *Luke 24:1–53* | The Magdalene goes to the tomb and finds that Jesus has risen!

- *John 20:1–18* | The Magdalene goes to the tomb and finds that Jesus has risen!

- *Luke 11:29–32* | THE SIGN OF JONAH: a metaphor for the resurrection of Jesus Christ.

- *Psalm 22:27* | One day everyone will remember the LORD.

Reflect

- Matthew, Mark, Luke, and John all share the story about Mary of Magdala at the empty tomb of the risen Christ. Why is this story repeated in all four Gospels?

- How do we build memories of Jesus in our life?

- How will you write your life story?

- What story are you going to write today?

Imagine

Today you have an invitation from Jesus. You are invited to go with Him to an art studio. Can you picture yourself holding His beautifully handcrafted invitation? The invitation is a work of art in and of itself! Please say YES.

Arriving at the studio, you learn that you and Jesus will both depict you as each sees you. After some encouragement, you begin. This is hard! Do you feel like you are making some mistakes? If so, you might try to cover them. Some of your choices are very nice, but overall, do you feel satisfied with your work and ready to show it off? You likely don't consider yourself an artist along the lines of a Leonardo da Vinci. Maybe it could be better. It's not perfect. Meanwhile Jesus works quietly, smiling as He goes. He seems pleased with His work.

When it is time for the big reveal, you show your self-portrait first. Tell Jesus what you depicted. Take time to tell Him how your artwork reflects your image of yourself. Describe the parts you like and the parts you wish were better.

What do you think will happen when Jesus shows you His artwork? Listen to Him tell you about His portrait of you. Notice how beautiful it is. It seems perfect!

Discuss why your self-portrait is different from His image of you. What is His explanation? Does He remind you that you were created in the image of God and wonderfully made by a Master Craftsman? Does He suggest that anyone who tells you otherwise does not deserve a voice in your life?

Leaving the studio, ask Jesus if you can trade your self-portrait for His. Leave yours behind. Stand tall in the truth of who you are in Christ and how wonderfully God created you.

I will give thanks to You, because I am awesomely and wonderfully made; Wonderful are Your works, And my soul knows it very well.

Psalm 139:14 (NASB)

Dare to Hope

Pouring Oil

Trust in him at all times, you people;
pour out your hearts to him, for God is our refuge.

Psalm 62:8 (NIV)

S ometimes trouble comes upon us all at once, and sometimes it takes its own sweet time to arrive. Trouble often feels like the jolt of an earthquake, followed by many rolling aftershocks.

"When trouble comes knocking on your door, don't answer!" That's what I said ever since my husband died unexpectedly. For a single mother in ancient times, with two sons, I faced trouble every day. My sons, Avi and Gili, were my dearest treasures and I did everything possible to protect and provide for them. I willingly sacrificed my own well-being for their benefit. It warmed my heart to see them beginning to live again, especially since the sudden death of their father, whom they admired and loved deeply.

Beloved as he was, my husband left us empty handed. As a follower of the prophet Elisha, he had devoted himself to spiritual matters and mostly overlooked financial matters.

The prophet, along with his followers, lived by the whims of good will and sometimes dedicated generosity of people they served. Our family honored my husband's devotion to God and did our best to live lives of faith and make do, one way or another.

Our stored provisions included flour, nuts, lentils, figs, honey, and olive oil. As the supplies continued to gradually diminish, I somehow managed to present satisfying meals day after day for our little family of three. I relished the creative skill of using whatever was available to craft satisfactory nourishment, but I knew trouble was coming. While Avi and Gili intended to follow in their father's footsteps and devote themselves to serving God and the prophet Elisha, they failed to learn a skill or trade to support themselves and their mother now in the absence of the prophet's support network.

One day while my sons were out looking for work and I was home alone, someone pounded heavily on my door. When I answered, he presented a legal complaint against my husband, now transferred to me, regarding an unpaid loan. The size of the debt surprised me, especially since I had no idea we were even in debt.

Furthermore, the lender asserted his legal right to take possession of both of my sons as slaves to settle the debt. How could I lose my husband AND both sons? The very thought was not only unbearable, but clearly unacceptable.

Given the surprise notice, I convinced the lender to return the next day. Plus, my sons were not home. As soon as the man left, I headed straight out to find Elisha and entreat him for help. I arrived to find him standing in prayer under the cool shade of a chestnut tree not far from town.

As I slowly but determinedly approached the prophet, he acknowledged my arrival.

"Talia."

He nodded, then raised his eyebrows to indicate that he was available and listening.

I wasted no time.

"Your servant, my husband, is dead. You know he revered the Lord, but now his creditor has come and demanded to take my two sons as his slaves."

I dropped to my knees and looked imploringly at Elisha. My heart was pounding, I was out of breath, and nearly faint with panic.

"How can I help?"

I was speechless. My mind was whirling and I had no idea how to answer.

Elisha took charge.

"Tell me, what do you have in your house?"

I was embarrassed to confess how low our supplies had fallen. Maybe I hoped that by ignoring it we wouldn't have to deal with it, or that we could continue to scrape by somehow. We had no money at all, and only one thing left to convert.

"Your servant has nothing there at all, except a small jar of olive oil."

It was our last. Just saying it aloud made it more real. The seeming finality of our dire straits was overwhelming.

Elisha nodded and thought for a moment. I thought I caught a glimpse of a smile before he commanded, "Go around and ask all your neighbors for empty jars, collect lots of empty clay jars. Then go inside your home and shut the door behind you and your sons. Pour oil into all the jars, and as each is filled, put it to the side and fill the next one."

I felt a little confused. How could my one small jar fill multiple jars? But, if we learned anything from following Elisha, we learned to trust and obey.

One time one of my husband's friends borrowed an axe to help cut some trees down by the Jordan River where they were building a meeting place. At one point, the ax head flew off the handle and sunk in the river. When he informed Elisha what happened, Elisha made the iron float so that he was able to recover it, finish the work, and not have to pay for losing what he borrowed.

Another time, Elisha told a man who had leprosy— Naaman the Syrian who served as commander for the king of Aram—to go wash seven times in the Jordan River. Although Naaman thought it was ridiculous and he didn't understand at first, he finally obeyed and was cleansed of his disease.

So, of course, I knew to trust God to speak and do miracles through Elisha. He was truly a man of God. Even so, as I ran home, I was thinking that my neighbors might think me crazy! If they had any idea how desperate we were, some might even feel bad giving me empty jars. Thoughts of faith mingled with reasons for doubt whirled around in my mind. My spirit rose and fell with each hurried step. But I determined to obey the prophet and trust God no matter what.

When I reached home, the boys greeted me with the bad news that their search for work proved fruitless once again. I informed them of all that transpired in their absence, including the lender's news about their father's debt, his demands for immediate payment or their lives turned over in servitude to him, as well as the instructions from the prophet. While the first words brought fear and dismay, Elisha's words seemed to offer them hope. We all dashed out and started knocking on doors.

As our neighbors responded, we took the jars and stacked them in the house and then went out again for more. When we could find no more empty jars available, we went home and closed the door behind us. We picked an empty jar and then I took the one small jar of olive oil we had left and held it over the empty one. We all looked at each other and then I started pouring.

Within in a few moments, we knew we were witnessing a miracle. Oil kept coming out of the little jar. More than could possibly have been in there. We watched in amazement as the oil continued pouring out until it filled the first empty jar. I set it aside and we selected another empty jar.

We watched as it filled, too. Then another. And another on and on. We were laughing and crying—hardly able to even believe what was happening. It was amazing!

The house soon filled with the rich fragrance of olive oil as we continued to fill jars, set them aside, and then start pouring oil into another empty jar. We worked together efficiently, each doing our part, while at the same time feeling a sense of wonder and incredible excitement. We felt hope.

We watched as the oil continued flowing from the little jar—the very same jar from the beginning—to fill every other empty jar in the house. When I noticed we had no more jars in waiting, I told Avi, "Bring me another one."

"There are no jars left."

Right then, just as oil reached the brim of that final jar, oil stopped pouring from our little jar.

We dropped to the floor and stared at one another. Then we just sat there for a few minutes looking at all the full jars stacked around the house. We realized we were surround by one of the most precious commodities in town.

Gili asked, "What next?"

I wasn't sure. Elisha didn't say and I didn't think to ask. So, I left the boys at home safely guarding the jars full of oil, closed the door behind me, and hurried back to the chestnut tree and found Elisha. I told him everything that happened and then asked, "Now what?"

He definitely smiled.

"Go, sell the oil, and pay your debts. You and your sons can live on what is left."

So, I obeyed. I went home and we got to work selling all the oil, then we returned all the borrowed jars to their original owners. Some neighbors even bought the oil and were delighted to have the opportunity to purchase such fine olive oil in their very own clay jars. After we finished, we counted out enough to pay my husband's debt and set that aside. When we realized how much was left, we cried great big tears of joy knowing that God had miraculously saved us from a terrible fate.

When the lender returned fully expecting to drag my boys away into his servitude, you should have seen his face after I let him restate his case and make his demands and then repaid the entire debt. He was completely shocked, and I think even a little mad. He couldn't believe it, and truthfully, we were still quite amazed ourselves.

As I closed the door behind him and turned to face Avi and Gili, I realized this was one of the best days of our lives. Then we knelt together in our home full of peace and joy and rejoiced in God's abundant blessings. Incredibly, in such a short span of less than a day or so, in conjunction with our daring hope and unquestioning obedience, God worked through Elisha to move us from an untenable circumstance of deep, dark despair to one of broad, bright hope for a much better future.

Explore

- *2 Kings 4:1–7* | The cupboard is bare, and the creditor is at the door.
- *2 Kings 6:5-7* | Elisha and the borrowed axe.
- *2 Kings 5:1-19* | Elisha and the leper Naaman.
- *2 Corinthians 4:7–9* | TREASURE: The Spirit fills us, just as the oil filled the jars.

Reflect

- Sometimes it's hard to ask for help. Why?

- Elisha asked the woman, "How can I help you?" If God asked you, "How can I help you?" what would you say?

- Why did Elisha ask the woman, "What do you have in your house?"

- If you were a clay jar, what treasure would be inside you?

Imagine

Hope, all by itself, is an elusive concept. When we try to capture a sense of hope, it seems to easily evaporate into nothingness. We feel great when we feel hopeful, and we feel empty when we don't.

What if God offered you a great big box of Hope? Despite its extra-large size it would be as light as a cloud. Would you want it? Would you accept it? Hold on, there is one condition: you cannot take the box with you. Once you accept the box of Hope, you will need to set it down and remember where you placed it. Are you willing to play along?

Picture yourself carrying your big box of Hope into an immense storage unit filled with shelves from floor to ceiling. There is plenty of space because all the shelves are empty!

Looking around, you see that each shelf has a label. The shelves by the door would be very convenient and it would be easy to remember where you placed your Hope. Do you want to place your box here for the sake of convenience?

The labels on these shelves by the door are: My Family. My Friends. My Network. But wait! Have family, friends, or your network ever failed you? Do you remember times when your hope in them led to disappointment?

Go further in and discover that there are shelves labeled: Religion and Spirituality. While these options are worthwhile, what assurance do they offer? They are helpful in tough times, but what do they give you when you have nothing left to give?

Deeper in the storage unit are more open shelves where you might place your big box of Hope: The Universe. The System. The Process. These nebulous entities are very trendy, but ask yourself if "The Process" has ever given you the hope of a more secure future? Are you willing to put your Hope in a trendy concept?

You might feel like giving up. Perhaps you've lost any hope of finding the perfect place for your big box of Hope. What if you finally see the place you have been searching for the whole time? In an instant you recognize that it's the right place. What do you think it is?

This shelf is labeled: God. There it is. That's the one! Do you think that this one surpasses all the other places where you might have placed your Hope? How might this be your best option? God says that hope in Him does not disappoint, because the love of God has been poured out within your heart through the Holy Spirit. (Romans 5:5 NASB)

Perhaps you realize now that in comparison to God, all the other places were only temporary holding spots. Will you leave your box of Hope with God? Take your time to think about it. You might feel hesitant to let go, but it will be simple and easy to remember where you placed it. It's with God.

As a bonus, if you leave your big box of Hope with God, He will give you a deposit slip to take with you in place of the box. The receipt, He tells you, will be a reminder of where you placed your Hope. He tells you that you have complete access to Hope whenever you want or need it. The Lord suggests that you carry your reminder close to your heart so that you never doubt that Hope in God is there for you, always. Hope will remain in your heart because you placed it with the One who loves you with His never-failing love. What will you do with your big box of Hope? Let's put our Hope in God and dare to hope!

Why, my soul, are you downcast?
Why so disturbed within me?
Put your hope in God,
for I will yet praise him,
my Savior and my God.

Psalm 42:11 (NIV)

For Further Study

A Promise Kept

Question: What is it like to live in Ur, 2000 BC?

"City of Biblical Abraham Brimmed with Trade and Riches," Andrew Lawler, 11 Mar 2016, *National Geographic*, Nationalgeographic.com/adventure/article/160311-ur-iraq-trade-royal-cemetery-woolley-archaeology

Question: What is the Ziggurat of Ur?

"Iraq's Answer to the Pyramids," Geena Truman, 23 Aug 2022, BBC, Bbc.com/travel/article/20220822-the-ziggurat-of-ur-iraqs-answer-to-the-pyramids

Question: Is there archaeological evidence of Ur and Haran?

"Top 10 Discoveries Related to Abraham," Brian Windle, 16 Jul 2021, Bible Archaeology Report, Biblearchaeologyreport.com/2021/07/16/top-ten-discoveries-related-to-abraham/

Serendipity

Question: Is a prayer shawl a tallit?

"What is a Tallit?" Leo Giosue, 18 Jun 2020, *The Jerusalem Post*, Jpost.com/special-content/what-is-a-tallit-631948

Two Sides of the Story

Question: What is the religious and cultural meaning for feet washing?

"Feet, Washing of," Emil G. Hirsch, Wilhelm Nowack, and Solomon Schechter, Jewish Encyclopedia, Jewishencyclopedia.com/articles/6051-feet-washing-of

God is Listening

Question: How big is the Tent of Meeting?

"Explore the Tabernacle in the Wilderness," Jack Zavada, 12 Aug 2019, Learn Religions, Learnreligions.com/the-tabernacle-700104

I Believe

Question: What is nard?

"What is Spikenard in the Bible?" Got Questions Ministries, Gotquestions.org/spikenard-in-the-Bible.html

Judgment Day

Question: What is a Pharisee?

"Who Were the Pharisees in the Bible?" Christianity.com, 21 Aug 2023, Christianity.com/jesus/birth-of-jesus/genealogy-and-jewish-heritage/how-were-the-pharisees-legalistic.html

The Troubled *Times* of Israel

Question: What is known about the life and times of Deborah?

"Deborah in the Bible," Robin Gallaher Branch, 29 Oct 2024, *Bible History Daily*, Biblical Archaeology Society, Biblicalarchaeology.org/daily/people-cultures-in-the-bible/people-in-the-bible/deborah-in-the-bible/

We Called a Meeting

Question: What did Mary and Martha serve for dinner?

"Foods and their Preparation for Eating," Fred H. Wight, Ancient Hebrew Research Center, Ancient-hebrew.org/manners/foods-and-their-preparation-for-eating.htm

Lost and Found

Question: Was it improper for the younger son to ask his father for his inheritance?

"Inheritance Practices in the First Century," Jirair S. Tashjian, *The Voice*, Christian Resource Institute, Crivoice.org/inheritance.html

Wait for It

Question: How is Hannah remembered today?

"5 Things You Didn't Know About Hannah in the Bible," Kristine Brown, 23 May 2024, Crosswalk, Crosswalk.com/faith/bible-study/5-things-you-didn-t-know-about-hannah-in-the-bible.html

Reaching Out

Question: How small is a mustard seed?

"What Does it Mean to Have Mustard Seed Faith?" Got Questions Ministries, Gotquestions.org/mustard-seed-faith.html

Out of the Shadows

Question: What is the Ceremony of Blessings and Curses?

"7 Facts Everyone Should Know About Mount Gerazim and Mount Ebal," Mordechai Rubin, Chabad-Lubavitch Media Center, Chabad.org/parshah/article_cdo/aid/4101198/jewish/7-Facts-Everyone-Should-Know-About-Mount-Gerizim-and-Mount-Ebal.htm

A Reversal of Fortune

Question: Is Ahinoam's hometown Jezreel connected to Armageddon?

"What is the Biblical Significance of Jezreel?" Got Questions Ministries, Compellingtruth.org/Jezreel.html

Dear Diary

Question: Who is the real Mary of Magdala?

"Mary Magdalene," Kristen Swenson, Bible Odyssey, Society of Biblical Literature, Bibleodyssey.org/articles/mary-magdalene/

The Magdalene

Question: What is my true image?

"Who Does God Say I Am?" Ken Boa, Reflections Ministries, Kenboa.org/spiritual-formation/who-does-god-say-i-am/

Dare to Hope

Question: Can olive oil represent the Holy Spirit?

"What was Olive Oil a Symbol of in the Bible?" Got Questions Ministries, Gotquestions.org/olive-oil-symbol.html

Imagination:
It's Not Just for Kids!

Special note from the author about Biblical storytelling and sanctified imagination

Photo by R. Lynn Lewis.

W e all tell stories. We talk about who we are, what we see, where we go, and what we do. Even a young child can tell a story. It is one of our most basic human forms of communication. It makes sense then, that our Creator God would choose to communicate with us in the form of a story in the book we call the Bible.

According to author and theologian Eugene Peterson, "The Bible turns out to be a large, comprehensive story, a *meta story*."[2] It contains a myriad of stories within the overall narrative, the classic "story within the story." The Bible is cohesive and consistent in its message and purpose. God has a story to tell us, and the story of the Bible "doesn't just tell us something and leave it there, it invites our participation. A good storyteller gathers us into the story. We feel the

---

[2] Eugene H. Peterson, *Eat This Book: A Conversation in the Art of Spiritual Reading.* Grand Rapids: Wm. B. Eerdmans Publishing Co., 2006, 40.

emotions, get caught up in the drama, (and) identify with the characters."3 This is the Bible, the word of God.

Why, then, do some of us struggle to stay awake when we read the Bible? Or find that our minds wander when we pray? It has been said that spiritually, we suffer from "malnourished imaginations."4 For many, the ability to imagine gradually diminishes over time as we grow up and mature. Factual information becomes the enemy of imagination, and this can have a devastating impact on our faith and relationship with God. If "worship is the imagination station"5 then we must engage our imagination when we worship.

The challenge some of us face is that our minds focus better on concrete information and "cannot focus well on abstractions."6 We rely on our five senses to experience reality in the physical world and find it more difficult to experience the reality of God in the spiritual realm.

Yet, this is where imagination—especially a sanctified imagination set apart for God's purpose—comes into play. According to author, pastor, and theologian Greg Boyd, "Everything we do in our spiritual lives will likely be enhanced if it is done with vivid mental images."7 He further notes, "The more concrete and vivid our mental images are, the more they are experienced as real and the more impacting they are in our

---

3 Ibid.

4 Justin Taylor, "Vanhoozer on Developing a Sanctified Imagination," The Gospel Coalition. US Edition, 3-8-2012. Thegospelcoalition.org/blogs/justin-taylor/vanhoozer-on-developing-a-sanctified-imagination. Accessed 2-24-2025.

5 James K. A. Smith. *You Are What You Love*. Grand Rapids: Brazos Press, 2016, xi.

6 Gregory A. Boyd, *Seeing is Believing: Experience Jesus Through Imaginative Prayer*. Grand Rapids: Baker Books, 2004, 92.

7 Ibid, 98.

life"[8] and "The central place where we experience spiritual realities is in the imagination."[9]

Pastor Ray Stedman says, "I hope you read your Bibles with what has been called the gift of sanctified imagination. The Bible is intended to be read that way-that you fill in some of the details with a bit of imagination and yet guided by the lines that are set forth in the stories involved."[10]

My writing endeavors to help readers engage in experiencing Bible stories as if we are there. Through spiritual eyes of imagination, I invite you to place yourself in the stories as if you are present—feel, hear, and see what the real people of a story may have felt, heard, and seen.

Biblical storytellers left "a lot of blanks in the narration, an implicit invitation to enter the story ourselves, just as we are, and discover for ourselves how we fit into it."[11] This is how we develop an intimate relationship with God, by seeing ourselves in His story.

"It isn't long before we find ourselves imaginatively... entering the story, taking our place in the plot, and following Jesus."[12] God invites us to journey with Him through His story as He journeys with us through ours. In this way, His loving presence and wise words can meet us as we enter His Word through the spiritual practice of sanctified imagination.

---

[8] Ibid.
[9] Ibid, 93.
[10] Ray Stedman, "Daring Daughters," Ray Stedman Authentic Christianity, message transcript and recording, 8-9-1964. Raystedman.org/thematic-studies/characters-in-scripture/daring-daughters. Accessed 2-24-2025.
[11] Eugene H. Peterson, *Eat This Book: A Conversation in the Art of Spiritual Reading*. Grand Rapids: Wm. B. Eerdmans Publishing Co., 2006, 42.
[12] Ibid. 48.

"Imagination" Bibliography

Boyd, Gregory A. *Seeing is Believing: Experience Jesus Through Imaginative Prayer*. Baker Books, 2004.

Peterson, Eugene H. *Eat This Book: A Conversation in the Art of Spiritual Reading*. Wm. B. Eerdmans Publishing Co., 2006.

Smith, James K. A. *You Are What You Love*. Brazos Press, 2016.

Stedman, Ray. "Daring Daughters." Ray Stedman Authentic Christianity, message transcript and recording, 8-9-1964. Raystedman.org/thematic-studies/characters-in-scripture/daring-daughters. Accessed 2-24-2025.

Taylor, Justin. "Vanhoozer on Developing a Sanctified Imagination." The Gospel Coalition. US Edition, 3-8-2012. Thegospelcoalition.org/blogs/justin-taylor/vanhoozer-on-developing-a-sanctified-imagination. Accessed 2-24-2025.

About the Author

Super Bowl family chapels, baseball stadium Bible Studies, church classrooms, Board rooms and C-Suites across the country—these are all places where Nico Richie traces the footsteps of her life and experiences that have helped shape her ministry and faith in Jesus Christ.

Nico first opened her heart to God as a high school student while living in New Jersey. She then moved south to Florida and graduated magna cum laude with a degree in Sociology from the University of Miami, where she also gained a strong foundation in her Christian faith.

Having moved west across the country to California she joined an interdenominational Christian ministry within the professional sports world where she focused on women's discipleship. During this time, she served on the pastoral staff of a community church to help equip members for ministry based on their spiritual gifts.

She subsequently moved to Texas and built a thriving consulting business, along with her husband, in which she specialized in personality-based solutions aimed at improving workplace satisfaction. She recently ventured into a writing group and began to explore and write about women in the Bible. She aims to equip women with Biblical tools that contribute to spiritual growth throughout life's journey.

The following three pillars of Scripture uphold Nico's lifelong call to ministry:

1. Then He said to His disciples, "The harvest is plentiful, but the workers are few. Therefore, plead with the Lord of the harvest to send out workers into His harvest." – Matthew 9:37–39 (NASB)

2. "You did not choose Me, but I chose you, and appointed you that you would go and bear fruit, and that your fruit would remain, so that whatever you ask of the Father in My name He may give to you." – John 15:16 (NASB)

3. "'But we will devote ourselves to prayer and to the ministry of the word.'" – Acts 6:4 (NASB)

Nico currently lives in the Houston, Texas area.

Order Copies

Amazon Paperback

Kindle eBook

To order a separate copy, use the appropriate QR code above.

Buy this copy

To buy this copy, visit the QR code link,
select "Buy Now" and input contact information,
then "Delivery Method" and "Event Purchase."

Made in the USA
Coppell, TX
29 May 2025

50000266R00098